Addiction Treatment
Escaping the Trap

ILLICIT AND MISUSED DRUGS

Abusing Over-the-Counter Drugs: Illicit Uses for Everyday Drugs

Addiction in America: Society, Psychology, and Heredity

Addiction Treatment: Escaping the Trap

Alcohol Addiction: Not Worth the Buzz

Cocaine: The Rush to Destruction

Dual Diagnosis: Drug Addiction and Mental Illness

Ecstasy: Dangerous Euphoria

Hallucinogens: Unreal Visions

Heroin and Other Opioids: Poppies' Perilous Children

Inhalants and Solvents: Sniffing Disaster

Marijuana: Mind-Altering Weed

Methamphetamine: Unsafe Speed

Natural and Everyday Drugs: A False Sense of Security

Painkillers: Prescription Dependency

Recreational Ritalin: The Not-So-Smart Drug

Sedatives and Hypnotics: Deadly Downers

Steroids: Pumped Up and Dangerous

Tobacco: Through the Smoke Screen

Illicit and Misused Drugs

Addiction Treatment
Escaping the Trap

by Ida Walker

Mason Crest

Mason Crest
370 Reed Road
Broomall, Pennsylvania 19008
www.masoncrest.com

Copyright © 2013 by Mason Crest, an imprint of National Highlights, Inc. All rights reserved. No part of this publication may be reproduced or transmitted in any form or by any means, electronic or mechanical, including photocopying, recording, taping, or any information storage and retrieval system, without permission from the publisher.

Printed in the Hashemite Kingdom of Jordan.

First printing
9 8 7 6 5 4 3 2 1

Library of Congress Cataloging-in-Publication Data

Walker, Ida.
 Addiction treatment : escaping the trap / Ida Walker.
   p. cm. — (Illicit and misused drugs)
 Includes bibliographical references and index.
 ISBN 978-1-4222-2427-4 (hardcover)
 ISBN 978-1-4222-2424-3 (series hardcover)
 ISBN 978-1-4222-9291-4 (ebook)
 1. Substance abuse. I. Title.
 HV4998.W35 2012
 616.86'06—dc23
                                            2011032551

Interior design by Benjamin Stewart.
Cover design by Torque Advertising + Design.
Produced by Harding House Publishing Services, Inc.
www.hardinghousepages.com

This book is meant to educate and should not be used as an alternative to appropriate medical care. Its creators have made every effort to ensure that the information presented is accurate—but it is not intended to substitute for the help and services of trained professionals.

CONTENTS

Introduction   6
1. What Is Addiction?   9
2. Addiction Treatment: A Brief History   35
3. Getting Help: Pharmacological Treatment of Addiction   65
4. Beyond Drugs: Nonpharmacological Treatment of Addiction   81
5. Staying Sober   107

Glossary   118
Further Reading   122
For More Information   123
Bibliography   124
Index   126
Picture Credits   127
Author/Consultant Biographies   128

INTRODUCTION

Addicting drugs are among the greatest challenges to health, well-being, and the sense of independence and freedom for which we all strive—and yet these drugs are present in the everyday lives of most people. Almost every home has alcohol or tobacco waiting to be used, and has medicine cabinets stocked with possibly outdated but still potentially deadly drugs. Almost everyone has a friend or loved one with an addiction-related problem. Almost everyone seems to have a solution neatly summarized by word or phrase: medicalization, legalization, criminalization, war-on-drugs.

For better and for worse, drug information seems to be everywhere, but what information sources can you trust? How do you separate misinformation (whether deliberate or born of ignorance and prejudice) from the facts? Are prescription drugs safer than "street" drugs? Is occasional drug use really harmful? Is cigarette smoking more addictive than heroin? Is marijuana safer than alcohol? Are the harms caused by drug use limited to the users? Can some people become addicted following just a few exposures? Is treatment or counseling just for those with serious addiction problems?

These are just a few of the many questions addressed in this series. It is an empowering series because it provides the information and perspectives that can help people come to their own opinions and find answers to the challenges posed by drugs in their own lives. The series also provides further resources for information and assistance, recognizing that no single source has all the answers. It should be of interest and relevance to areas of study spanning biology, chemistry, history, health, social studies and more. Its efforts to provide a real-world context for the information that is clearly presented but not overly simplified should be appreciated by students, teachers, and parents.

The series is especially commendable in that it does not pretend to pose easy answers or imply that all decisions can be made on the basis of simple facts: some challenges have no immediate or simple solutions, and some solutions will need to rely as much upon basic values as basic facts. Despite this, the series should help to at least provide a foundation of knowledge. In the end, it may help as much by pointing out where the solutions are not simple, obvious, or known to work. In fact, at many points, the reader is challenged to think for him- or herself by being asked what his or her opinion is.

A core concept of the series is to recognize that we will never have all the facts, and many of the decisions will never be easy. Hopefully, however, armed with information, perspective, and resources, readers will be better prepared for taking on the challenges posed by addictive drugs in everyday life.

— *Jack E. Henningfield, Ph.D.*

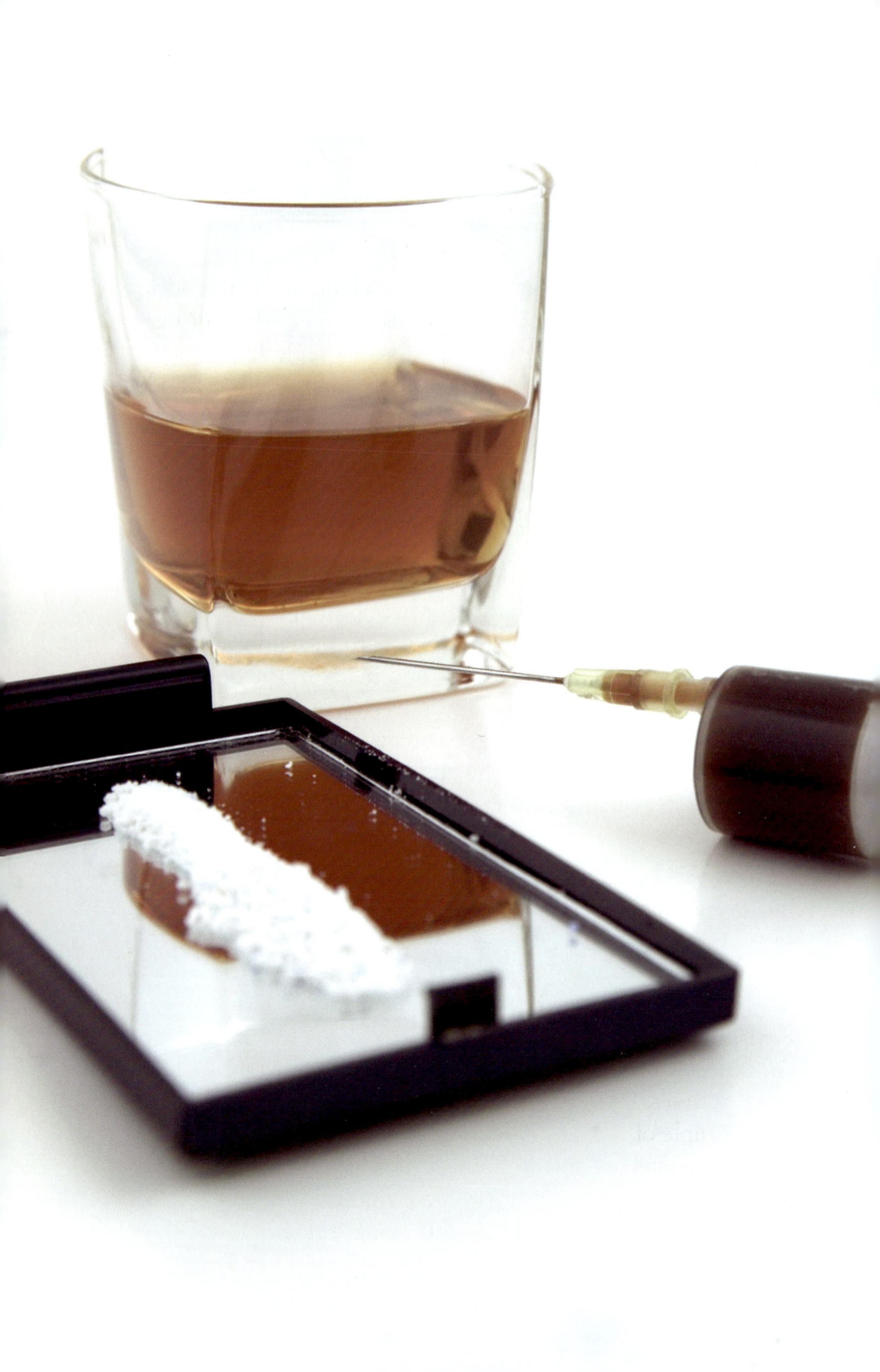

1 What Is Addiction?

So many meth addicts out there don't believe it is possible to face the rest of their lives without Meth.... Well, I'm here to say it can be done. I am living proof that there can be a better life on the other side of being a "meth-head."

Near the end of my three-year run, I was a daily smoker. I ran for days with very little if any sleep and very little nutrition. I was homeless on the streets. That is, of course, when I wasn't in jail. Not a friend in the world and my family had given up on me for their own sanity. I had been arrested for possession and sales twice, arrested for shoplifting and stealing, for altering the plates on my car, for driving without insurance and for a dirty "UA" [urine analysis].... I was given 10 years probation and received a $10,000 fine and a threat from the judge whom I had been before so many times, that if I ever came before him again I was guaranteed a couple of years in prison, no questions asked.

I was arrested at work twice and must have had 20 jobs in that three-year period. I had to drive more than 40 miles away to find a job since no one in town would hire me. I had so many sexual encounters that it should have been deemed a death wish.

Unprotected sex with HIV drug users, that if I didn't get HIV or AIDS, I could have easily become pregnant or be infected with Hepatitis.

That was five years ago. Today I am in my last year of college to get my Bachelor's Degree in Addiction Studies. My goal after graduation is to become an Addiction Counselor. . . . I guess what I am trying to say is, if I can turn my life around at age 35, then it is within the reach of anyone who truly wants it.

It hasn't been easy by any stretch of the imagination, it's been a long, hard road and still even after five years I have "using dreams" and miss my old way of life. I fight the cravings each and every day, but I have come to a place in my life where I realized I had much more to offer this world than being a drug addict. Maybe, just maybe, I can help one other addict realize this as well, and then my life in *purgatory* will have meant something.

The story above was written by Sheka K. on the website www.anonymousone.com. She became addicted to **methamphetamines**, lived to tell about it, and is now in the midst of recovery. For those like Sheka who choose to live life without addiction, they'll find that recovery is a lifelong process with no definitive endpoint. Still, most find it well worth the time and effort.

Addiction: A Definition

When a drug is taken into the body, it creates a reaction. When a prescription or over-the-counter drug is taken as instructed by a health-care professional or according to

Methamphetamine is a very addictive stimulant drug. In its crystalline form, shown here, it is known as crystal meth, ice, and glass.

the product label, the effects can be anticipated and are usually desired. After all, these medications are taken to treat a medical condition. However, when someone takes these chemicals in ways or amounts contrary to their intended use, **adverse** effects can occur, including dependence, which is also referred to as addiction.

The definition of addiction has changed over the years. It was originally used in **pharmacology** in reference to the tolerance-inducing qualities of some drugs and substances. If something has tolerance-inducing qualities, the body gets used to having the substance in its system. When this occurs, the individual must take increasingly larger amounts of the drug to achieve the original effect. This older definition emphasized the **physiological** aspects of taking drugs.

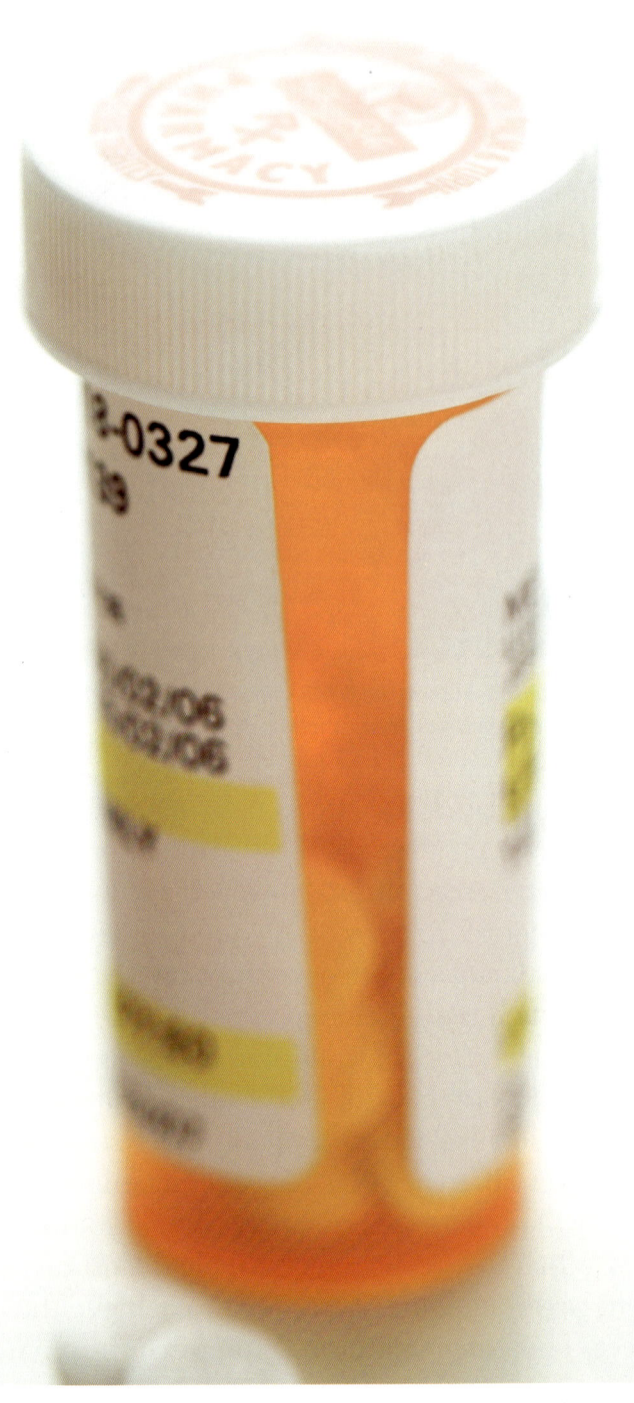

Drugs cause chemical reactions within the body. Doctors anticipate these reactions and use controlled amounts of certain prescription drugs to treat medical conditions.

Meanwhile, the psychological world put the emphasis for its definition on the compulsive, chronic, relapsing behavior of drug use. This definition for addiction was broader, and it included drugs such as cocaine and marijuana before it was recognized that these drugs too could cause physiological dependence. Similarly, from the perspective of most ordinary people, addiction referred to someone's **propensity** to keep abusing a substance even though it was clear that it was not good for them.

Today, the medical and scientific communities make distinctions between physical dependence and psychological dependence (or addiction). The medical, scientific definitions are **relatively** narrow. Someone who is physically dependent on a substance will suffer a syndrome of physiologic and behavioral responses should she stop taking the drug suddenly—or go "cold turkey." These responses—called withdrawal symptoms or simply withdrawal by the American Psychiatric Association—are specific to the drug class and are often opposite in nature to the effects produced by the drug. For example, the constipation caused by morphine is replaced by severe diarrhea, the muscle relaxation caused by alcohol can be replaced by tremors or even convulsions, the agitation caused by stimulants is replaced by sleepiness, the alertness produced by nicotine is replaced by difficulty concentrating. Of course people differ in their specific reactions, but in general, they tend to follow similar patterns that are related to the drug they were taking. (For more information on withdrawal symptoms from the various drugs of abuse, see the National Institute of Drug Abuse website, drugabuse.gov)

Addiction Treatment—Escaping the Trap

Someone who is dependent or addicted to a substance has an uncontrolled, compulsive need to use the drug or other chemical substance. Some general characteristics of addiction are:

- impaired control over drug use
- compulsive use
- continued use despite harm
- craving

Not all medical professionals agree on a definition of addiction, however. It was once believed that only *psychoactive* drugs that crossed the *blood–brain barrier* could be considered addictive. These drugs would temporarily change the brain chemistry, giving the person a period of euphoria—the high or rush sought by those abusing drugs. Today, many people want to add activities such as gambling, food, sex, and pornography to the list of addictive substances.

Proponents of this way of thinking claim that people participating in these behaviors experience a "high." They cite studies showing that the *hypothalamus* produces *peptides* when people participate in such activities, just as it does when people use an addictive chemical substance. They further argue that *endorphins* released into the brain when people gamble, eat, or view pornography, among other addictive behaviors, positively reinforce the behavior of the person with a problem with these activities. Proponents of this theory also claim that when someone addicted to such behaviors suddenly stops, withdrawal symptoms are encountered, just as they are when someone stops abusing an addictive drug.

If an individual is physically dependent on a drug, then he will experience withdrawal symptoms, such as headaches, if he stops taking the drug suddenly.

Addiction Treatment—Escaping the Trap 15

In the past only drugs that altered the body physically were considered to be addictive. Now the definition of addiction is being expanded to include activities such as gambling, eating, and pornography.

Not everyone in the medical field believes that activities such as those listed above are truly addictive. Opponents of the idea that activities can cause addictions do not dispute the fact that people who have problems with those activities face withdrawal-type effects when they are unable to participate in them. Their contention, however, is that the effects are symptomatic of a behavior disorder, not true addiction.

The term "addiction" does not appear in the *Diagnostic and Statistical Manual of Mental Disorders* (DSM-IV TR, the most recent release). Instead, this psychiatric manual lists dependence and withdrawal symptoms of

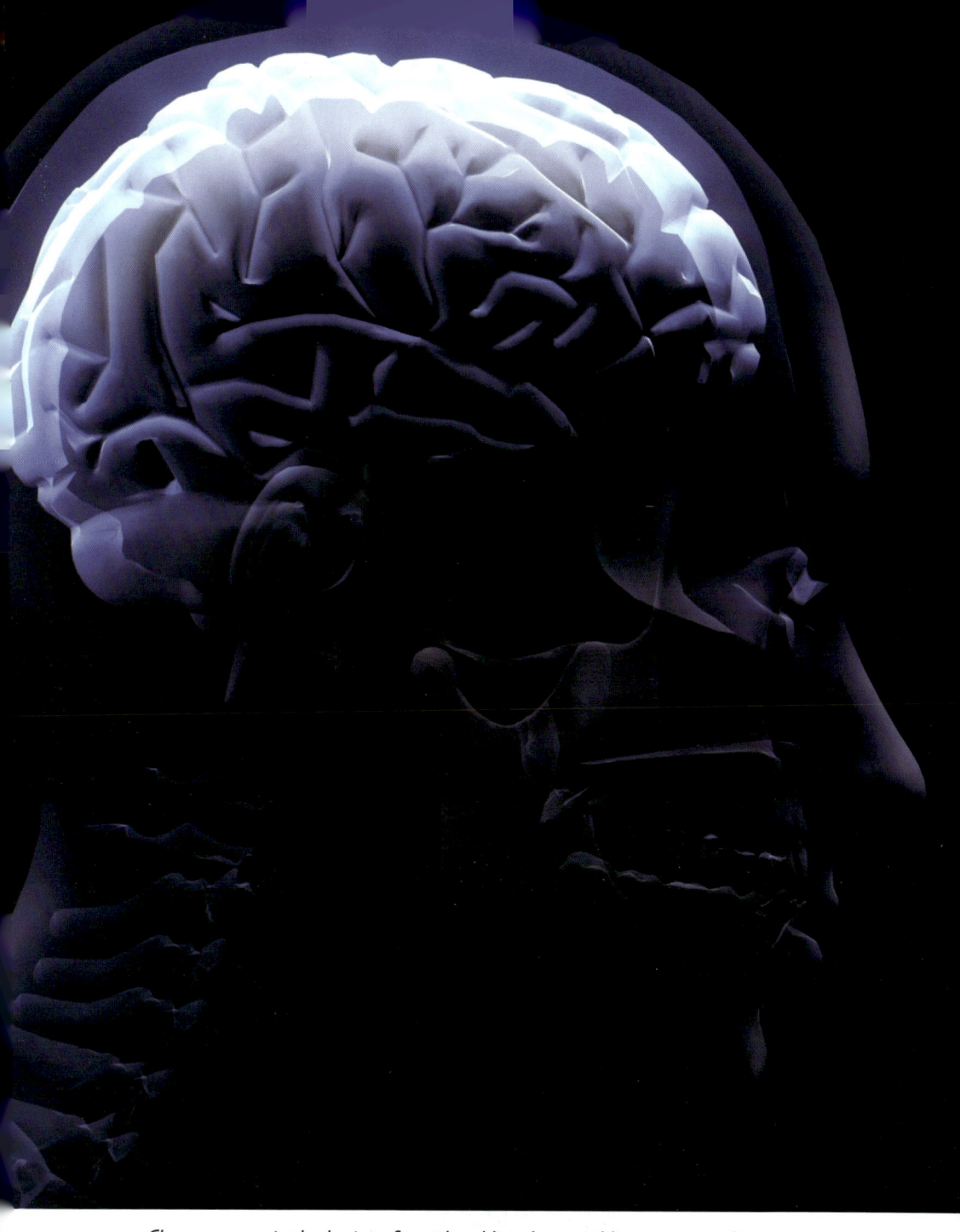

Changes occur in the brains of people addicted to gambling or eating. Opponents of the idea that these activities are addictive argue that these people have behavior disorders, not addictions.

Addiction Treatment—Escaping the Trap 17

drugs. The DSM also describes substance abuse disorder. More people experience this condition than dependence, although some will escalate to dependence.

The arguments over vocabulary and definitions are likely to continue, but one thing is certain: no matter how you define addiction, it clearly can have both physiological and psychological aspects.

Physiological Dependence

As mentioned earlier in this chapter, physical dependence means that the body will go through withdrawal symptoms when the substance is removed. Not all drugs and other chemical substances that produce physiological dependency are addictive. For example, **cortisone**, **beta-blockers**, some laxatives, nasal decongestants, and many antidepressants cause a physical dependency but are not addictive. (Although not all prescription drugs are addictive, none should be stopped suddenly without the guidance of a health-care professional.)

Psychological Addiction

Human nature makes one want to repeat behaviors that bring pleasure and avoid those that do not. The person who abuses a substance does so despite oftentimes knowing that he is doing something harmful, perhaps even life threatening. But the psychological need to abuse the substance to obtain that pleasurable feeling outweighs any risks. It can be as hard, and is sometimes harder, to break this psychological bond than it is to break the physical dependence on the substance.

Not everyone agrees on the definition of addiction, but the trend among mental-health experts is not to distinguish between addiction and dependence. Whatever their definition, all psychiatric experts agree that this is a serious problem that is deeply rooted in the lives of those who struggle with it.

How People Become Addicted

Someone doesn't just wake up one day and decide she is going to develop an addiction or dependency before she goes to bed that night. Addiction doesn't work that way; it is a process, not a spur-of-the moment decision. For

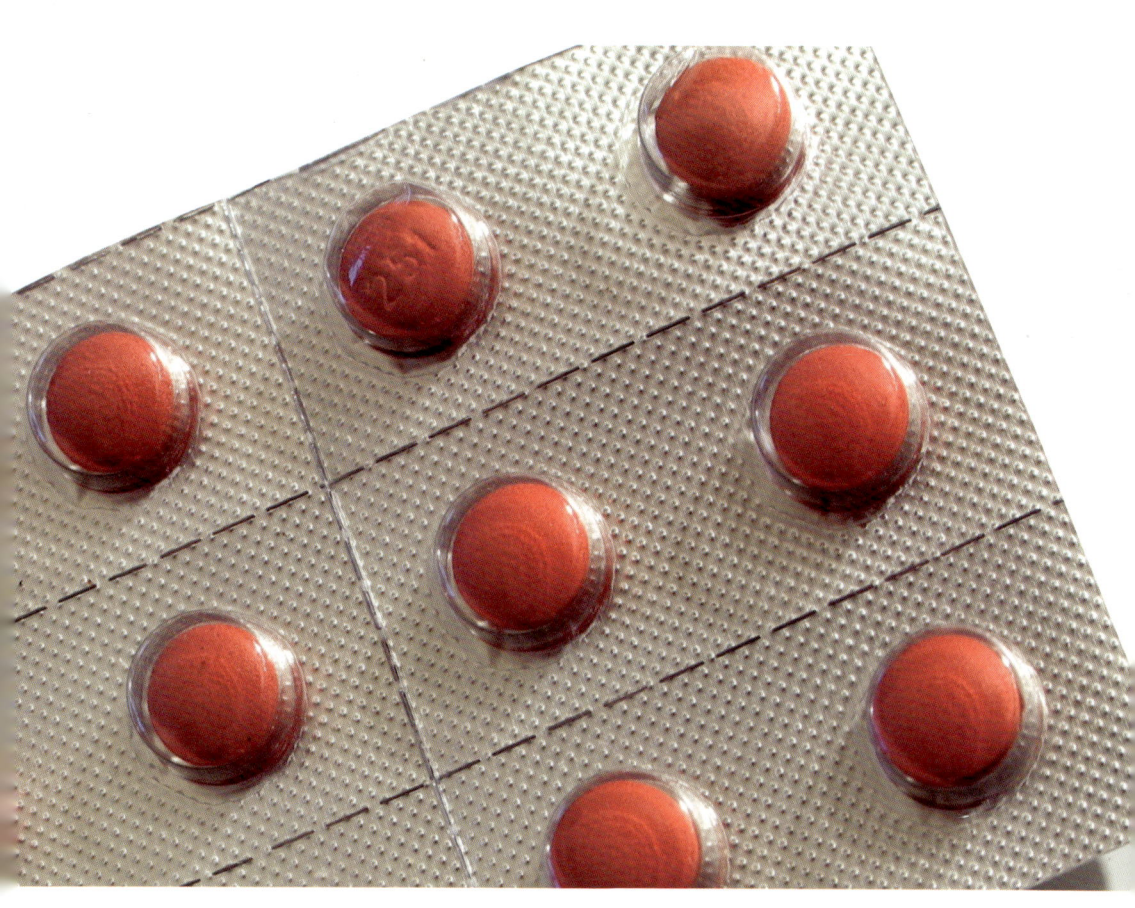

Some drugs, such as nasal decongestants, can cause physical dependency but not psychological addiction.

It is human nature to want to repeat a behavior that provides pleasure. This is why many people crave chocolate; eating it makes them happy.

most people, using drugs—including alcohol, tobacco, and prescription and over-the-counter medications—is not a physical or psychological problem when used sparingly. For other people, the drug or other substance becomes the overwhelming force driving all of their actions. These people may have started out using drugs in moderation, but gradually, their life becomes centered on getting and using the substance being abused.

Why one person develops an addiction to a substance while another person using the same substance does not

A person does not decide to form an addiction. The process usually happens gradually, until one day he can no longer face life without chemical help.

Addiction Treatment—Escaping the Trap 21

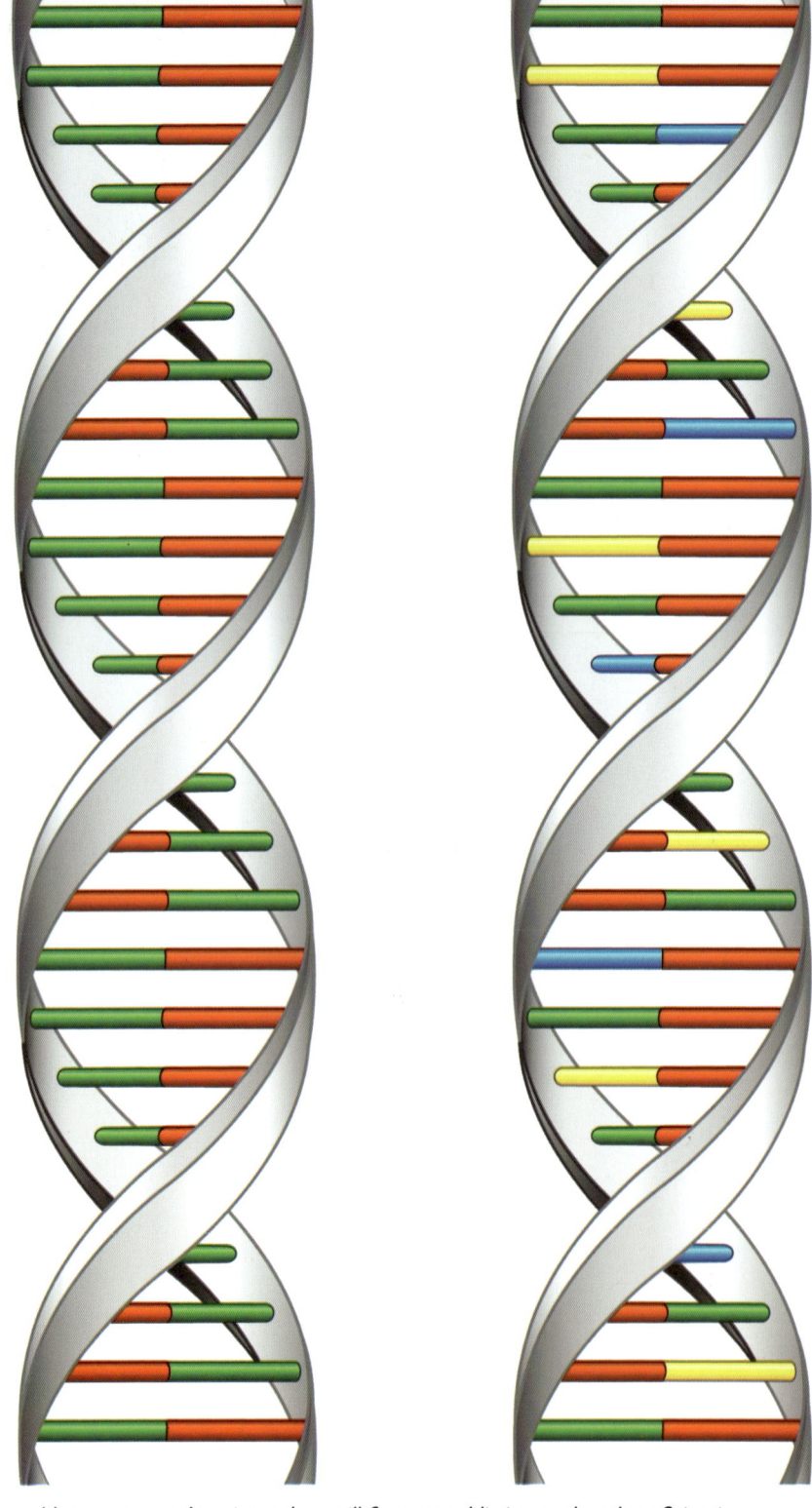

Not everyone who tries a drug will form an addiction to that drug. Scientists think that DNA may play a role in deciding whether or not someone becomes an addict.

22   Chapter 1—What Is Addiction?

remains a mystery. Some researchers believe that a genetic *predisposition* may contribute to addiction, especially to alcohol. This doesn't mean that the child of an alcoholic will definitely become an alcoholic, just that there might be an increased chance that this could happen, especially if environmental circumstances contribute to addiction's likelihood.

Addiction, for some people, arises out of a need to find a way to deal with stress. Ours is a fast-paced, highly competitive world, and some people turn to a chemical substance to help them relax, to numb their emotions, or to provide them with an escape from their troubles. While some people might find help through yoga, meditation, and other relaxation techniques, others will turn to alcohol, tobacco, and other substances.

The teenage years are a time of exploration. Adolescents learn about both themselves and the world around them. It's not uncommon in North American culture for that exploration to include experimenting with drugs. If the teen's *peer group* includes individuals who abuse drugs, the possibility of drug use increases. For some, experimenting with drugs is short lived; for others, it will signal the beginning of a life of addiction.

How an individual deals with drugs and alcohol is a learned behavior. In other words, someone teaches individuals the behaviors that lead to addiction.

Addiction and Families

Our parents are the first, and in many ways most important, teachers we will ever have. If parents abuse alcohol, tobacco, or other drugs, that behavior becomes part of a child's environment; he may come to believe that getting drunk or high is the only way to deal with unpleasant

Adolescence is a time of testing boundaries and exploration. For many teenagers this includes experimenting with drugs.

situations or even to celebrate joyous occasions. Substance abuse can become a pattern of everyday life.

Even parents or siblings who take prescriptions according to instructions can facilitate drug abuse in teens. Some of the fastest-growing drugs of choice for young people are prescription drugs. Many homes have at least one type of prescription medication in their medicine cabinets, making it easily available for abuse. Teens and

Drug Approval

Before a drug can be marketed in the United States, the Food and Drug Administration (FDA) must officially approve it. Today's FDA is the primary consumer protection agency in the United States. Operating under the authority given it by the government, and guided by laws established throughout the twentieth century, the FDA has established a rigorous drug approval process that verifies the safety, effectiveness, and accuracy of labeling for any drug marketed in the United States.

While the United States has the FDA for the approval and regulation of drugs and medical devices, Canada has a similar organization called the Therapeutic Product Directorate (TPD). The TPD is a division of Health Canada, the Canadian government's department of health. The TPD regulates drugs, medical devices, disinfectants, and sanitizers with disinfectant claims. Some of the things that the TPD monitors are quality, effectiveness, and safety. Just as the FDA must approve new drugs in the United States, the TPD must approve new drugs in Canada before those drugs can enter the market.

young adults may be under the misconception that because the medication is approved by the U.S. Food and Drug Administration (FDA) or the Therapeutic Product Directorate (TPD) in Canada and is prescribed by a health-care professional, that it is safe for everyone to use. That is a potentially fatal misunderstanding.

Addiction and Friends

Next to parents, peers are probably the most important influences on a teen's life. Peer group influence becomes more important as the child evolves away from the core family and prepares to enter the adult world. As mentioned earlier, involvement with a peer group that emphasizes drug abuse can make that behavior seem commonplace and a way to be popular. Most people want to have friends, and for some teens, drinking alcohol, smoking, or abusing drugs is their way of finding that popularity.

Addiction and the Media

Then there's the media. Any time you turn on the television, watch a movie, surf the Net, or listen to popular music, you'll encounter references to drugs, alcohol, and tobacco. Young people spend hours in front of computers and television sets, so they end up absorbing the all-too-prevalent message: drugs, alcohol, and tobacco are means for having fun or dealing with stress and other life conditions.

Signs of Addiction

Some people can use alcohol and other substances without much of a problem. They know when to stop and how much they can handle. When they aren't using the substances, they suffer no withdrawal symptoms.

So how can you tell if an individual has a problem with substance abuse or addiction? In many cases, it depends on the type of drug being used. Here are some common signs of substance abuse:

- change in friends; hanging out with a new group
- reclusive behavior—long periods spent in self-imposed isolation
- long, unexplained absences
- lying and stealing
- involvement on the wrong side of the law
- deteriorating family relationships

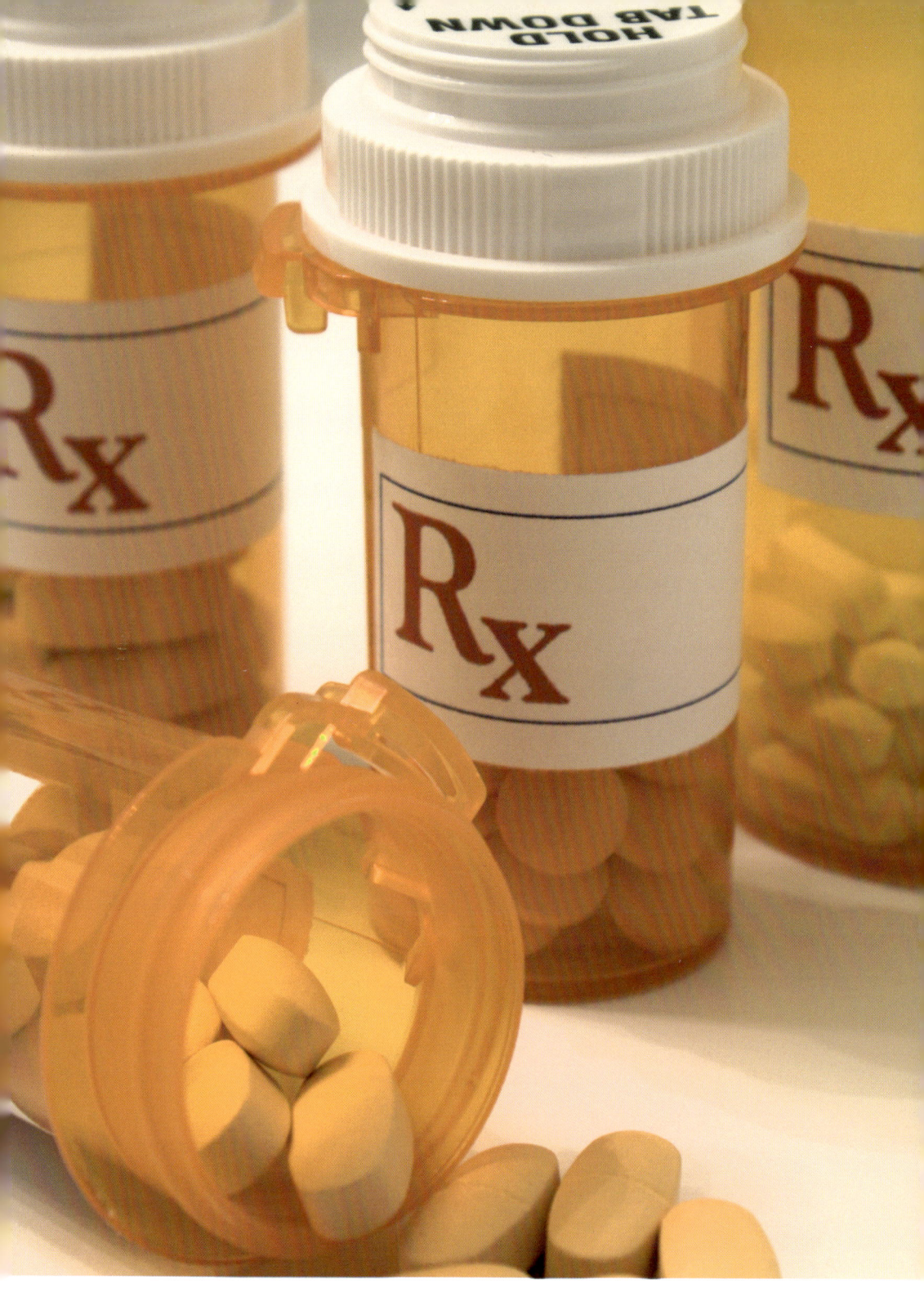

Prescription drugs have become popular drugs of choice for young people. Teens may incorrectly think that these drugs are safer than illegal drugs.

Addiction Treatment—Escaping the Trap 27

According to Veterans Affairs Canada (www.veterans.gc.ca/clients/sub.cfm?source=health/wellness/9), someone may have a problem with drugs if they:

- drink alcohol or use drugs in secret
- suffer blackouts
- have headaches or hangovers
- consume quickly and more often.

The problem may be addiction if any of the following can be answered by yes:

- Are you having problems with any part of your life? Physical health? Work? Family? Mental health? Your social or spiritual life?
- Do you know when to stop drinking? Do you often drink too much and become intoxicated? Do you binge drink?
- Do you have withdrawal symptoms such as shakiness, irritability or seizures when you stop drinking or using drugs?
- Are you using illegal drugs or having your drugs prescribed by more than one doctor?
- Has your drug use increased since you first started using them?
- Are you spending more and more time thinking about where the money for your next drinks or drugs will come from?

- obvious intoxication, delirious, incoherent or unconscious
- changes in behavior and attitude
- decrease in school performance

Exhibiting any of those characteristics doesn't always mean that someone has an addiction or substance abuse problem. However, they are warning signals that should be taken seriously.

Starting and Stopping

Except in extremely rare cases (and television shows and movies), most people who become addicted to a substance do so on their own; no one forces them to take—or keep taking—a drug or to drink alcoholic beverages. This fact leads many with substance addiction to believe they can also beat their addiction on their own. After all, if they started smoking . . . or drinking . . . or using drugs, then they should be able to stop. Right? Sadly, the answer is usually, "Wrong." This attitude generally results in repeated failures at *sobriety*, at least in the long run.

But why *can't* individuals conquer addiction on their own? If the drug use has only occurred for a short time,

Nicotine Addiction

More teens are addicted to nicotine (the chemical found in cigarettes and other tobacco products) than are addicted to any other substance. Nicotine addiction lacks many of the symptoms discussed in this chapter; for instance, if you're addicted to nicotine, chances are your school performance won't go down. You won't become "high" or intoxicated; it probably won't have a major effect on your relationships. But that doesn't mean that nicotine addiction isn't real or that it isn't serious.

According to the National Institute on Drug Abuse (NIDA):

Addiction is characterized by compulsive drug seeking and use, even in the face of negative health consequences. It is well documented that most smokers identify tobacco use as harmful and express a desire to reduce or stop using it, and nearly 35 million of them want to quit each year. Unfortunately, only about 6 percent of people who try to quit are successful for more than a month.

What's more, according to NIDA, tobacco is the leading preventable cause of death in the United States.

If a person does not seek help for his addiction and learn to cope with the cravings, he is likely to relapse.

they often can. The longer an individual has been addicted to the substance, however, the greater the likelihood that he cannot permanently abstain from using the substance without the help of some kind of a treatment program.

Researchers studying drugs and addiction have discovered that when drugs are used over a long period, serious changes occur in how the brain functions. Some of these changes, including the felt need to continue using the substance, can continue long after the person has stopped taking the drug or substance. If the individual has not learned ways to cope with the continuing cravings to use the drug or substance, she is all-too likely to *relapse*.

The drug's long-term effects on the brain are not the only factors that can doom an individual's attempts at sobriety, however. For many people addicted to drugs and alcohol, the entire drug-taking experience is a time to socialize with friends. Some individuals do not have the strength to stand up to their friends, family, or cowork-

Another obstacle to sobriety is the social aspect of drug use. Often a recovering addict has friends who also use drugs, and it is hard to be the only one not participating.

ers, and be the only one not using drugs or alcohol. It's not easy to be the only one not doing something. Peer pressure, especially when combined with changes the substance might have caused in the brain, can make **abstinence** a nearly impossible war to win.

Regardless of how addiction is defined and caused, one thing has been proved repeatedly: people battling drug dependence and addiction need help to break free.

Abuse—or Misuse?

Abuse and misuse are two different things; unfortunately, both can lead to addiction.

Misuse:

Patients may forget or not understand their prescription's directions. They may start making their own decisions, perhaps upping the dose in hopes of getting better faster.

Abuse:

People may use prescription drugs for nonmedical reasons. Prescription drug abusers may obtain such drugs illegally and use them to get high, fight stress, or boost energy.

Substance Abuse vs. Dependence

The American Psychiatric Association's DSM-IV defines substance abuse differently from dependence. More young adults would fall into the substance abuse category, which is also a serious condition that can escalate into dependence (what many people think of as addiction).

DSM-IV Substance Abuse Criteria

Substance abuse is defined as a maladaptive pattern of substance use leading to clinically significant impairment or distress as manifested by one (or more) of the following, occurring within a twelve-month period:
1. Recurrent substance use resulting in a failure to fulfill major role obligations at work, school, or home (such as repeated absences or poor work performance related to substance use; substance-related absences, suspensions, or expulsions from school; or neglect of children or household).
2. Recurrent substance use in situations in which it is physically hazardous (such as driving an automobile or operating a machine when impaired by substance use).
3. Recurrent substance-related legal problems (such as arrests for substance related disorderly conduct).
4. Continued substance use despite having persistent or recurrent social or interpersonal problems caused or exacerbated by the effects of the substance (for example, arguments with parents or friends about consequences of intoxication and physical fights).

DSM-IV Substance Dependence Criteria

Dependence is a maladaptive pattern of substance use leading to clinically significant impairment or distress, as manifested by three (or more) of the following, occurring any time in the same 12-month period:

1. Tolerance, as defined by either of the following:
   (a) A need for markedly increased amounts of the substance to achieve intoxication or the desired effect or
   (b) Markedly diminished effect with continued use of the same amount of the substance.
2. Withdrawal symptoms
3. The substance is often taken in larger amounts or over a longer period than intended.
4. There is a persistent desire or unsuccessful efforts to cut down or control substance use.
5. A great deal of time is spent in activities necessary to obtain the substance, use the substance, or recover from its effects.
6. Important social, occupational, or recreational activities are given up or reduced because of substance use.
7. The substance use is continued despite knowledge of having a persistent physical or psychological problem that is likely to have been caused or exacerbated by the substance (for example, current cocaine use despite recognition of cocaine-induced depression or continued drinking despite recognition that an ulcer was made worse by alcohol consumption).

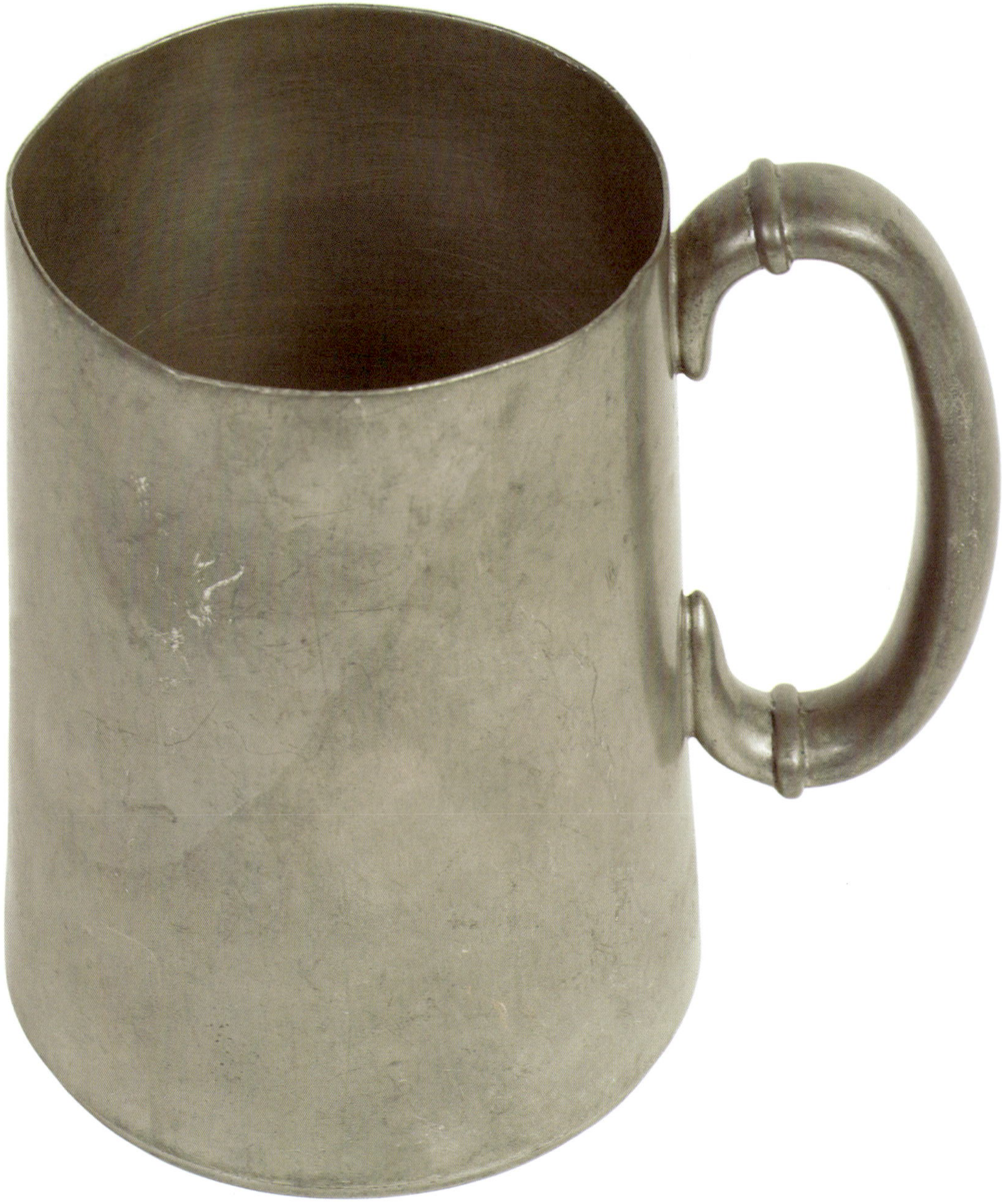

2 Addiction Treatment: A Brief History

Addiction has been around almost from the first time someone discovered that a substance could make one get a "high." Eventually, it became apparent that those "good times" came with a price. That price was addiction and all the negative effects that went with it—illness, poverty, violence, crime, death. Although the problem of addiction was acknowledged, its causes were not understood, however, and that fact was reflected in how those with substance addiction were treated.

Treatment: The Early Days

The view that addiction is a disease has not always been the dominant belief. Historically, many in American society have considered people with substance-abuse problems to be morally weak and lacking self-control. In many cases, individuals suffering from those problems were deemed to be hopeless and sent to prisons or asylums. Other North Americans believed that only prayer could beat the demons of addiction.

Amid what many would consider to be the dark ages of addiction treatment, an enlightened individual began working on behalf of individuals with mental disease and addiction. In the late eighteenth century, Benjamin Rush encouraged the understanding of "inebriety," the term he used for alcoholism. He believed it to be a medical condition and encouraged using medical methods to treat it.

The incidences of addiction Benjamin Rush witnessed were just the beginning. During the late nineteenth and early twentieth centuries, the number of people abusing alcohol and drugs such as cocaine, **ether**, opium, morphine, **bromides**, and nicotine increased dramatically. Historian Harry Levine calls that period America's

Addiction was not always treated as a disease. In the past, many individuals were sent to prison because of their problems.

Benjamin Rush

Benjamin Rush (1746–1813) was one of the most important figures in the early days of U.S. history. At the forefront of addiction treatment and in the treatment of the mentally ill, he also practiced bloodletting as a medical treatment. Rush was an activist in the antislavery movement and opposed capital punishment. He pushed for more and better education for women and for free public schools.

Born in Philadelphia, Rush attended schools there and in Maryland. In the fall of 1766, he went to Scotland to study medicine. Scotland was then the center of medicine, and Rush excelled in the environment. After two years, he had earned his medical degree.

After leaving school in Scotland, he traveled to London, where he attended lectures and had the opportunity to meet such important figures as Benjamin Franklin, Sir Joshua Reynolds, and Samuel Johnson. After a trip to Paris, Rush returned to Philadelphia and, at age twenty-three, became the first chemistry professor in America. He also established a thriving medical practice and organized the first antislavery society in America, the Pennsylvania Society for Promoting the Abolition of Slavery and the Relief of Negroes Unlawfully Held in Bondage. He became friends with political figures Thomas Paine, John Adams, and Thomas Jefferson. It was Benjamin Rush who suggested that Paine title his pamphlet on American independence *Common Sense*. Rush was one of the signers of the Declaration of Independence.

During the War for Independence, Rush served as the surgeon general of the Middle Department of the Army. He resigned his commission when his efforts to improve the conditions at military hospitals were unsuccessful.

Of his many accomplishments in the field of medicine, many historians cite as his most important one the reforms he established in the care of individuals with mental illness while he was the senior physician at Pennsylvania Hospital. According to Rush's biographer, Carl Binger, he replaced the cruelty and indifference that had characterized treatment in the past with compassion. Instead of relying on treatment methods that had in the past been used in the treatment of mental illness, Rush stressed clinical observation. In 1812, Rush published the first U.S. textbook on psychiatry, *Medical Inquiries and Observations upon the Diseases of the Mind*.

In recognition for his work in medicine, some of his former students established a medical college named after him in Chicago. His importance in the field of psychiatry is evident as well; his portrait appears on the official seal of the American Psychiatric Association. In 1965, the organization placed a bronze plaque on his grave. It calls him the Father of American Psychiatry.

"discovery of addiction." Increased usage and its **concomitant** problems, along with the pioneering work of Benjamin Rush, led to the establishment of facilities dedicated solely to the treatment of addiction. One of the first such homes was organized as part of the Washingtonian movement.

The Washingtonian Movement

In 1840 Baltimore, six gentlemen—William Mitchell, David Hoss, Charles Anderson, George Steer, Bill M'Curdy, and Tom Campbell—met in a bar (called a tippling house then) to drink and have a good time. One night, a renowned **temperance advocate** was speaking at a church in town. Intrigued, two members of the group were sent to hear his speech. The members returned with favorable impressions of both the speaker and his message. The tavern keeper overheard the discussion and flew into a rage. He called all temperance lecturers hypocrites. A heated argument ensued between the men and the innkeeper, getting hotter and louder with each passing minute. Finally, the men decided that they would give up drink and become the Washingtonian Total Abstinence Society, the Washingtonians. That very night they pledged complete abstinence from all forms of alcoholic beverages.

Needless to say, these newly reformed men had to find a different place to meet. The following night, they met in a carpenter shop, and each man brought a new member. During the almost nightly meetings, members would stand before the assembly and confess their personal battles with alcohol. This became the forerunner of such self-help organizations as Alcoholics Anonymous (AA).

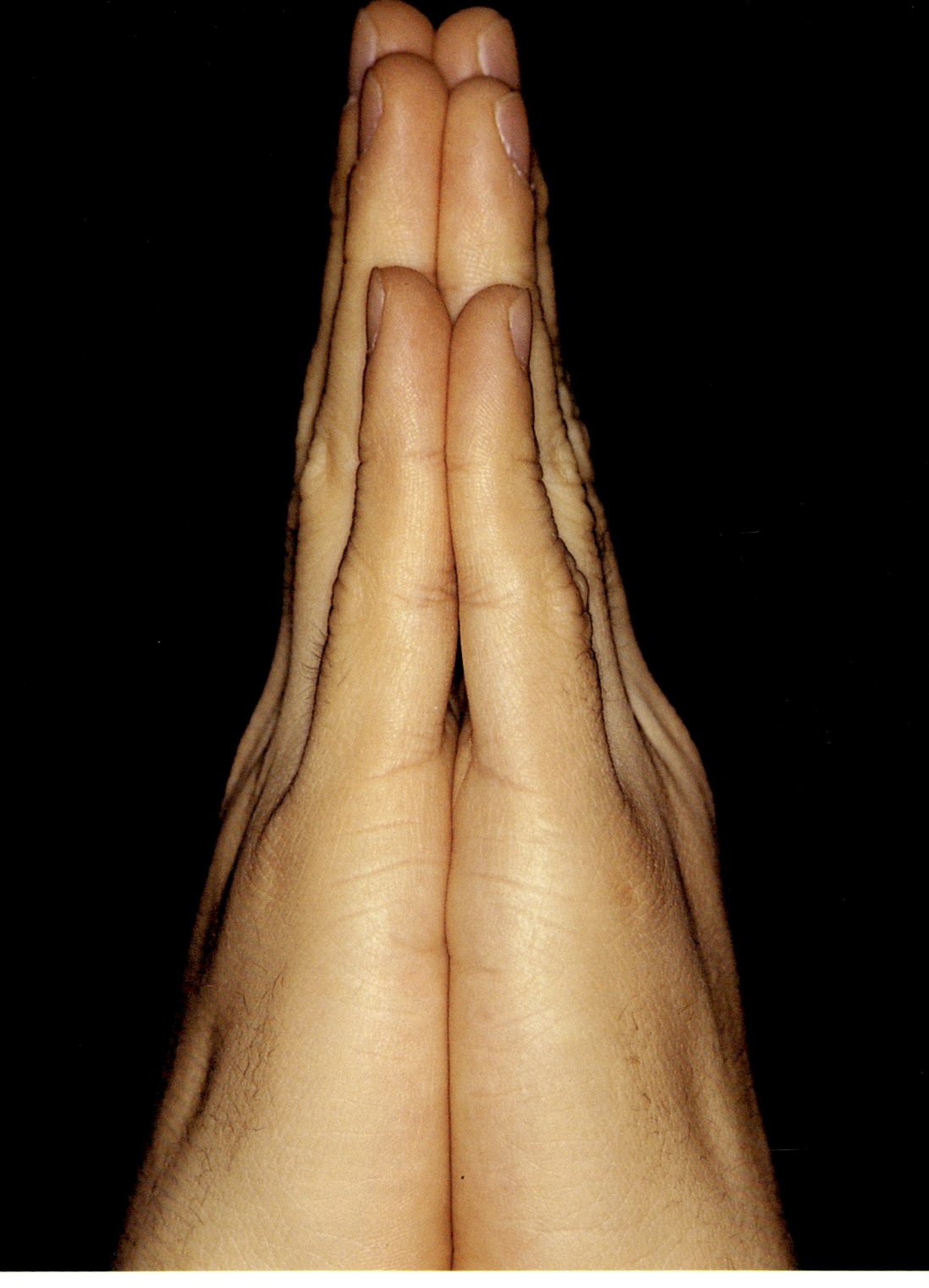

In the past people with addictions were thought to be morally weak. Some Americans felt that prayer was the only way to conquer the demons of addiction.

Addiction Treatment—Escaping the Trap

Benjamin Rush established important reforms in the care of individuals with mental illness. He stressed clinical observation and compassion over cruelty and indifference.

The reputation of the group spread first in the city of Baltimore, and then throughout the country. Eventually, most major cities (and several smaller ones) across the United States had their own chapters of the Washingtonians.

In many ways, the Washingtonian movement was unique. Its members were those most in need; individuals with drinking problems made up the bulk of the organization's membership rolls. It was also a classless organization, with no distinction made between the haves and have-nots. Writing about the Washingtonians in 1878, the Reverend W. H. Daniels noted:

> It was quite a wonderful thing to hear a man in plain clothes, and without any of the graces of speech, declare what had been done for him, and *exhorting* with all simplicity and boldness that others should give up liquor as he had done.

The Washingtonian Movement advocated total abstinence from alcohol. Ironically, the Washingtonians got their start in a tavern.

Addiction Treatment—Escaping the Trap

The common people heard these men gladly, and drunkards by the thousands and tens of thousands signed the total abstinence pledge.

In this movement there was no exception made in favor of the man who could buy fifteen gallons over the man who could buy a single glass.

No matter what the individual's background was, each had pledged to give up alcoholic beverages completely. Each man was expected to do so on his own, buoyed by the distressing tales told at meetings of the evils wrought by alcohol consumption.

Alcohol consumption statistics indicate that the early years of the temperance movement met with success in reducing the amount of alcohol use. According to Reverend Daniels' 1848 book, in 1831, every man, woman, and child drank an average of six gallons of some alcoholic beverage; by 1840, consumption had been cut in half. Once the Washingtonians got involved, temperance moved more quickly throughout the country, with more than 100,000 "drunkards" alone signing the pledge, according to Reverend Daniels. Those whose addiction to alcohol was less severe added thousands to the pledge rolls of the Washingtonian movement. While the exact number of individuals who became members of the Washingtonians is unknown, some historians believe that at its peak, membership may have been as high as 300,000.

Although one of the founding ideas behind the Washingtonian movement was that each individual had the ability to beat alcohol addiction on his own, it became evident that some could not. For individuals who could not conquer their addiction to alcohol without help, the Washingtonians opened and operated a few *"inebriate*

Women and the Fight for Temperance

Prohibition came along at the right time. In the early 1800s, though women still did not have the right to vote, they were becoming active in issues that affected them, their families, and society as a whole. In the minds of many women, one of the biggest threats to the well being of those around them was liquor, and they were ready to fight—both literally and figuratively. Until the late 1800s, women were on the fringes of involvement in the temperance movement, but with the formation of the Women's Christian Temperance Union (WCTU) in 1874, women's efforts on behalf of temperance took center stage.

The WCTU exemplifies a characteristic of many organizations of the period: it was not limited to one "cause." The organization saw alcohol as a result of bigger social issues, and under the leadership of Frances Willard, it took on other issues of social conscience, including a better American Indian policy, prison reform, better sanitary conditions, and civil service reform. The WCTU never forgot the original purpose of its founding, however, and concentrated on teaching the public, including children, about alcohol and the dangers of inebriation. The WCTU joined with McGuffey's Readers to educate children about the evils of licensing liquor stores. Every state except Arizona had compulsory temperance education in their schools by 1902, largely through the efforts of this partnership.

One of the most recognizable names associated with the WCTU is Carrie Nation. She traveled throughout the United States and into Canada and the British Isles fighting to eliminate the existence of saloons. Almost six feet tall, the sight of her with an ax, ready to demolish single-handedly any saloon, made many men quake in their shoes.

Though not as well known today, the WCTU still exists. Members are still required to pledge to a life of abstinence from alcohol and other substances. Today's WCTU fights against drug abuse, tobacco use, and continues to educate against alcohol use and abuse.

homes," including ones in Boston, Massachusetts, and Chicago, Illinois. Operating under the belief that out of sight meant out of mind, these homes helped individuals keep a distance from alcohol.

More Than a Kettle and a Bell

Although today it might be associated mostly with its Red Kettle drives and disaster response efforts, the Salvation Army has a long history that includes rehabilitation of individuals with alcohol addiction.

In 1865, poverty was rampant in the East End of London. Driven by a need to reach out to these individuals, Methodist minister William Booth and his wife, Catherine, formed an organization called the Christian Mission to preach to the "unchurched" people living there. It soon became apparent to Booth and his followers that they could not meet an individual's spiritual needs if material needs were not met as well. So, in addition to telling the people about Jesus, they fed and sheltered the homeless, and offered opportunities to kick the habit to those addicted to alcohol.

The group's name was changed to the Salvation Army in 1878, and its ministers were given army rankings rather than the traditional title "reverend," a structure unique to the organization. (Reverend Booth became known as General Booth.) From its world headquarters still located in London, the Salvation Army operates in more than one hundred countries, and its message is spread in more than 160 languages.

The programs first developed by General Booth are still offered today. The Salvation Army has, however, adapted to a changing society. In addition to rehabilitation and residential programs for those fighting alcoholism, it also operates day-care centers, AIDS educational and assistance programs, services for the aging population, and medical facilities. And proceeds from the Red Kettle drives help bring happier holidays to families in need, as well as help support year-round projects.

When the Washingtonian movement was founded, great strides were made to avoid anything of a controversial nature, including religion. As the movement grew, however, so did the topics its members pursued, and the movement became involved in nontemperance social reforms. These included *sectarian* religion, politics, and *abolitionism*. Controversy over such issues led to internal arguments among the movement's membership and the eventual *demise* of the movement.

Although traits of the Washingtonian movement are echoed in such support programs as AA, the organization itself soon vanished from North Americans' memories. Other groups that supported abstinence had more staying power. One of them, the Women's Christian Temperance Union (WCTU), still exists, though its members have expanded their interests to other areas in addition to alcohol.

Among the lessons learned through the experiences of the Washingtonian movement is that individuals

Women were an important part of the temperance movement beginning in the late 1800s. The Women's Christian Temperance Union tackled temperance as well as other social issues of the time.

Those in favor of temperance viewed alcohol as evil. Alcohol and the bars that served it were going to cause the destruction of youth.

46 Chapter 2—Addiction Treatment: A Brief History

usually *cannot* kick the alcohol habit by themselves. In some cases, additional support comes from religion or at least a belief in a higher power. In others, *psychotherapy* plays a role.

The Emmanuel Movement

In November 1906, a group of individuals with functional illnesses met at Boston's Emmanuel Episcopal Church. Under the guidance of Reverend Elwood Worcester and Reverend Samuel McComb, this meeting would grow into the first experiment in treating alcohol addiction by combining individual and group therapy. Its success in treating individuals addicted to alcohol by using **depth psychology** and religion in a systematic manner brought it acclaim from all over the country.

Unlike founders of previous groups who attempted to keep religion out of their organizations (such as the Washingtonians), Reverend Worcester believed that the church had a responsibility toward those who were both physically and mentally ill. In Reverend Worcester's mind, treatment was not an either-or—medicine or religion—issue. He believed that medical practitioners and clergy should work together toward treatment.

Reverend Worcester's Emmanuel Movement entailed three components: group therapy classes, individual therapy conducted by the clergy at a church-based clinic, and personal visits conducted by what Reverend Worcester called "friendly visitors."

The Emmanuel Movement became so successful that its facilities couldn't keep up with those seeking assistance. So the movement also developed training programs to prepare other clergy to work with health-care providers in the care of those in need. Practitioners came from many different religions, moving beyond the founding Episcopal faith.

As with most early treatment programs, alcohol addiction was most often treated by this group. Individuals with addictions attended the movement's classes along with those suffering from other illnesses. In many ways, the classes were like church services; passages were read from the Bible, hymns were sung *a cappella*, and prayers were offered on behalf of those in need. But these classes also dealt with the practical side of addiction. Lectures included discussions on neurology and psychology, as well as on how to deal with anger, anxiety, and grief, among other topics. Attendees were also given suggestions on changes they could expect when living a sober life. A *social hour* generally followed all classes, giving everyone a chance to get to know each other.

Although the classes were integral to the Emmanuel Movement's treatment plan, the clinic was where the real therapy took place. Each participant had to complete a thorough physical examination before being accepted into the program. In some cases, a psychological examination was required as well, and if a *psychosis* was diagnosed, the individual was not allowed to participate.

Reverend Worcester believed that for alcohol addiction treatment to be effective, individuals had to come in every day. During these daily sessions, the idea of staying sober was implanted in the individual; practices necessary to maintain the habit of living a sober life were instilled in the person, hopefully replacing the habits of living one clouded by alcohol.

During these therapy sessions, the person would divulge any information that might have a bearing on his

Women had felt the effects of alcohol addiction for centuries, since alcohol addiction contributed to domestic abuse and poverty. In the nineteenth century, women banded together to fight alcoholism in a movement that was also connected to the women's rights movement.

Addiction Treatment—Escaping the Trap 49

Reverend Worcester advocated daily therapy sessions that focused on maintaining the habit of a sober life. Hypnosis was also sometimes part of the process.

addiction. Physical, social, psychological, moral, and spiritual avenues were examined; nothing was off limits. Through this process of analysis, the individual could better understand what had led him to addiction, and through this enlightenment, how he could achieve and maintain sobriety.

Prayer and relaxation also played important roles during clinic sessions. Practitioners of the Emmanuel Movement's techniques believed that strengthening an individual's spiritual life through prayer would make him stronger and better able to fight alcohol addiction and relapse. Relaxation through the use of light hypnosis was also used in the clinic. In his book *Understanding and Counseling the Alcoholic*, Howard J. Clinebell Jr. writes that an individual was

> invited to be seated in a reclining chair, taught to relax all his muscles, calmed by the soothing words, and in a state of physical relaxation and mental quiet the unwholesome thoughts and untoward symptoms are dislodged from his consciousness, and in their place are sown the seeds of more health-giving thoughts and better habits.

Through the process of treating many alcoholics, Reverend Worcester developed an insight unique for his time, as quoted in Clinebell's book:

> The analysis, as a rule, brings to light certain experiences, conflicts, a sense of inferiority, maladjustment to life, and psychic tension, which are frequently the predisposing causes of excessive drinking. Without these, few men become habitual drunkards. In reality, drunkenness is a result

of failure to integrate personality in a majority of cases. Patients, however darkly, appear to divine this of themselves, and I have heard perhaps fifty men make this remark independently: "I see now that drinking was only a detail. The real trouble with me was that my whole life and my thought were wrong. This is why I drank."

While Reverend Worcester and other clergy were tending to the spiritual needs of the alcoholic, and healthcare professionals looked after their physical and mental needs, the friendly visitors of the Emmanuel Movement acted not as professionals but as friends. Though they tried to make certain that the recovering alcoholic was following the prescribed program, perhaps their most important duty was to provide a sympathetic ear ready, willing, and able to listen.

One group of people proved to be very effective friendly visitors—other alcoholics. After all, who could understand better what the newly recovering alcoholic was going through, physically and emotionally? Being a friendly visitor also had a side benefit: helping someone else though the **travails** of living a sober life reinforced sobriety in the visitor.

The Emmanuel Movement was very successful, and that success played a significant role in its demise. The numbers of individuals seeking help for addiction and other ailments from Emmanuel Movement services led to a shortage of trained practitioners. Though efforts were made to train individuals in the movement's methods, it couldn't occur quickly enough, and many individuals had to be turned away.

The movement depended on the cooperation between the medical community and the clergy. At first,

The Emmanuel Movement included spiritual help from clergy, physical care from physicians, and emotional support from "friendly visitors." Other recovering alcoholics were especially effective visitors.

Addiction Treatment—Escaping the Trap

Alcoholism was fought from various perspectives in the nineteenth and twentieth centuries. Some considered it a spiritual problem, others a medical disease. Still others attempted to deal with it legally, treating it as a crime. It was this perspective that led to Prohibition. In this photo, taken in the 1920s, police officers watch while liquor is poured down the drain.

that wasn't a problem, and the cooperation was seen as being mutually beneficial. As the Emmanuel Movement's methods began to demonstrate increasing **efficacy** in the treatment of addiction, however, a professional rivalry began to heat up. Instead of working *with* the movement's leaders to find a solution, many in the medical community began to work and speak out *against* the movement and its practices. Because the movement depended so much on the cooperation of health-care professionals, it could not withstand the changing tide of medical thought.

Another factor in the ultimate failure of the Emmanuel Movement was the changing public attitude toward addiction, especially toward alcoholism. During much of the nineteenth century, alcoholism and other drug addictions were seen as treatable illnesses. As a result, treatment centers and programs such as those established by the Emmanuel Movement, often based on religion,

54 Chapter 2—Addiction Treatment: A Brief History

This nineteenth-century "cure" for alcoholism simply replaced one addiction with another!

Addiction Treatment—Escaping the Trap

The Keeley Cure

In the mid- and late nineteenth century, one of the most popular treatments for alcohol, drug, and nicotine abuse was the Keeley Cure, developed by Dr. Leslie E. Keeley. Treatment consisted primarily of injections of a bichloride of gold (a gold molecule combined with a chloride molecule), from which it earned its nickname the "Gold Cure." The original Keeley Institute was opened in Dwight, Illinois, in 1879. By the end of the 1890s, every state had a Keeley institute for the treatment of people with addictions. At its peak, there were more than 200 Keeley treatment centers across the country.

Claims of being cured were soon heard from graduates of the program. People who had beaten their addiction with the Keeley Cure served as walking advertisements for the success of the program. Or so it seemed.

One of the lesser-known parts of the Keeley Cure was the use of group therapy in the treatment process. In all likelihood, the group therapy portion of the cure was what actually produced the favorable results in those undergoing treatment by the Keeley Cure. By the turn of the century, the claims of cure by gold had been disproved. An editorial in the February 28, 1900, Nebraska State Journal read:

> The medical profession generally attributes the cure of drunkenness devised by the late Dr. Keeley to the imagination of the patients. They claim that his method was pure quackery, that there was absolutely no therapeutical effect from injections of the alleged "chloride of gold," but that his treatment was purely of the mind, one of the branches of "faith cure" or healing by laying on of hands.

At any rate, after having a great vogue and bringing much money into the purse of the inventor of the "cure," the fad gradually died away and the various establishments where the hocus pocus had been conducted with so much seriousness, were closed one after another until the "gold cure" is a reminiscence.

were established. But as the nineteenth century came to a close, attitudes changed; no longer were individuals with addictions simply people with "unsavory" but treatable illnesses. According to researcher William White, the prevailing attitude became one of seeing addicts as criminals, morally *reprehensible* individuals: "Let those currently addicted to alcohol and other drugs die off, and prevent the creation of new addicts through the vehicles of moral *suasion* and the legal prevention of the non-medical use of psychoactive drugs." Many considered people with addictions a drain on the economy, and some discouraged the use of public funds in helping them.

Public attitudes were also influenced by *ethics* scandals surrounding false claims of a cure for addiction, such as the Keeley Cure. There was also no standardized scientific method to prove the efficacy of the treatments, so public *skepticism* grew.

By 1917, the Emmanuel Movement had fallen victim to forces inside and outside the organization and ceased to operate. Its influence still runs through addiction treatment, however, especially in twelve-step recovery programs such as Alcoholics Anonymous.

The Twelve Steps of Alcoholics Anonymous

After the failed government experiment called *Prohibition*—the ultimate in trying to end alcohol abuse—and the passage of the Harrison Anti-Narcotic Act of 1914, attitudes toward individuals with addictions again shifted. The most profound shift back to the philosophy that addiction could be treated occurred with the founding of Alcoholics Anonymous (AA).

AA didn't just suddenly appear out of nowhere. The Washingtonians' influence is evident in the program, and AA's use of sponsors is not unlike the friendly visitors of the Emmanuel Movement. Perhaps the biggest influence on the founders of AA—Bill Wilson and Bob Smith—was the Oxford Group and its founder, Frank N. D. Buchman.

In 1934, stockbroker Bill Wilson (perhaps better known as Bill W. in keeping with AA's policy of anonymity) was introduced to the Oxford Group by a childhood friend and fellow alcoholic, Ebby T., who had become involved with the organization when introduced to it by another drinking friend. Bill W. was immediately attracted by the group's requirements that members:

- make *restitution* to anyone they had harmed.
- conduct a self-analysis, noting any "personal defects."
- confess their personal defects to another person.
- open themselves up to direction from God by using prayer and meditation.

During his numerous tries at sobriety, Bill W. had turned to doctors and spiritual advisers for help. From one doctor he learned that alcoholism wasn't a sign of moral weakness; it was an illness, much like an allergy. From spiritual advisers, he learned that some alcoholics had been successful in finding sobriety through a personal relationship with a higher power and through self-examination, much like that conducted through the Oxford Group.

In 1935, Bill W. met Bob Smith (Dr. Bob), a surgeon from Ohio, who was also dealing with alcoholism. With much in common, they quickly became friends. They read and studied Bible passages as well as the principles of the Oxford Group. On June 10, 1935, in Akron, Ohio, Dr. Bob reportedly took his last drink. That date is also considered the birth date of Alcoholics Anonymous, though the official name would not come about for another four years with the publication of *Alcoholics Anonymous*, better known as *The Big Book*. This highly successful organization was formed by the bonds that had developed between these two men based on their battles to leave an alcoholic lifestyle behind them.

AA has grown to become the best-known and most successful program for helping people who have problems with alcohol; how the program works is discussed later in this book. Today, there are more than 100,000 chapters located all over the world. AA's books and pamphlets are published in more than thirty languages.

The Oxford Group

Frank N. D. Buchman was a Lutheran minister from Pennsylvania. A controversial figure, he seemed to always find ways to antagonize people. In 1908, after resigning from the hospice for homeless boys and young men he had founded (he had an argument with the trustees over money), he traveled to Europe. While in England, he formed A First Century Christian Fellowship, an organization based on the premise of changing the world one person at a time. During meetings called "house parties," individuals knelt and testified about the horrors addiction to alcohol, drugs, and tobacco had brought to their lives.

What began very small grew into the international organization Buchman called the Oxford Group. In 1938, Buchman renamed the group Moral Re-Armament (MRA), reflecting the political climate surrounding the re-militarization of Germany following World War I. (In 2001, the group would be renamed yet again. It is now known as Initiatives of Change.)

Buchman's interfaith group was based around four absolutes:

1. honesty
2. purity
3. unselfishness
4. love

The group's goal was to change human will to conform to that of God. By doing so, thereby making the world act together.

The original organization has given birth to support organizations dealing with other forms of addiction. These include Narcotics Anonymous, Gamblers Anonymous, and Cocaine Anonymous. Each organization is based on the original twelve steps as formulated in AA:

1. We admitted we were powerless over alcohol—that our lives had become unmanageable.
2. Came to believe that a Power greater than ourselves could restore us to sanity.
3. Made a decision to turn our will and our lives over to the care of God as we understand Him.

Alcoholics Anonymous was founded on June 10, 1935 by Bill Wilson and Bob Smith. The birthday is also the day that Dr. Bob took his last drink.

AA and other addiction treatment groups like it are built on a twelve-step program. Each step represents an important part in the progression toward sobriety.

4. Made a searching and fearless moral inventory of ourselves.
5. Admitted to God, and to ourselves, and to another human being the exact nature of our wrongs.
6. We're entirely ready to have God remove all these defects of character.
7. Humbly asked Him to remove our shortcomings.
8. Made a list of all persons we had harmed, and became willing to make amends to them all.
9. Made direct amends to such people wherever possible, except when to do so would injure them or others.
10. Continued to take personal inventory and when we were wrong promptly admitted it.
11. Sought through prayer and meditation to improve our conscious contact with God as we understand Him,

praying only for knowledge of His will for us and the power to carry that out.
12. Having had a spiritual awakening as the result of these steps, we tried to carry this message to drug addicts and to practice these principles in all our affairs.

Programs have also been devised for the people whose lives are affected by someone with alcoholism. AA recognizes the importance of family and friends to the person as she adjusts to life as a recovering alcoholic. Al-Anon

Family and friends are very important in the process of recovery. AA recognizes this, and two programs, Al-Anon and Alateen, offer help to this important support system.

62 Chapter 2—Addiction Treatment: A Brief History

A serendipitous side effect of drug treatment is the reduced likelihood that the individual in treatment will be involved in criminal activity while in treatment and for a time after. Studies have shown that criminal activity among opioid abusers is decreased by as much as 50 percent when they participate in a methadone treatment program. (Read more about methadone in chapter 3.) The "clean" addict isn't out looking for ways to score his next hit, often by committing crimes. He is also better able to get and keep a job, another factor leading to decreased crime rates by individuals in drug and alcohol treatment.

and Alateen operate as support groups for friends and families, helping those involved with the recovering alcoholic deal with the changes, as well as realize they are not alone on their journey.

Treatment: Does It Work?

Many studies have been conducted on the efficacy of drug treatment, and most have found that programs can reduce drug use by 40 to 60 percent.

How well a treatment program works depends on several things, including the dedication of the individual seeking a life in recovery and the support she receives from the people in her life. Today's treatment methods for addiction to alcohol and other substances take much from the historical precedents presented in this chapter. Spurred by the proven benefits of treatment programs in general, drug and alcohol treatment also takes advantage of new discoveries about addiction and treatment, including the benefits of drug therapy.

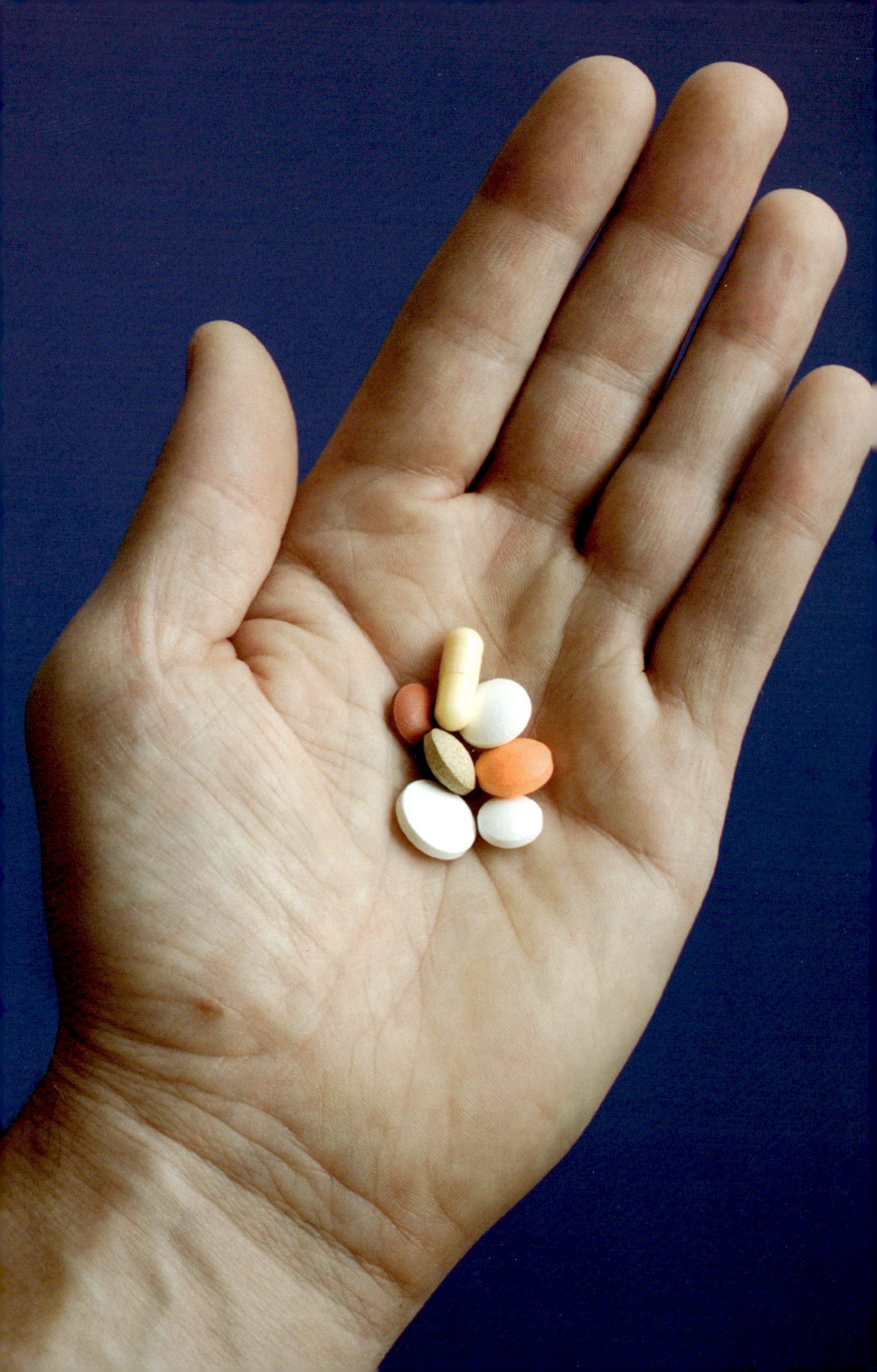

3 Getting Help: Pharmacological Treatment of Addiction

For someone kicking a substance abuse problem, the early days of withdrawal can bring with them physical symptoms as the body goes through a **detoxification** process. Sometimes, these symptoms might make the individual question the benefits of doing so.

The type and severity of withdrawal side effects can depend on the substance being abused, how long the individual used the drug, how much of the drug was taken, and even the age of the person addicted to the substance. Some of the more common withdrawal side effects include heavy sweating, nausea and vomiting, extreme headaches, body pain, and even **delusions**.

Medications can be used to help alleviate many of the side effects of withdrawal. But, that's not the only role pharmacology plays in the treatment of substance abuse addictions. The use of medications has proven to be an effective treatment *protocol* for many—but not all—addictions.

Alcohol Addiction

Medications can be effective in treating alcohol addiction. ***Opioid antagonists*** reduce the intoxicating effects—the buzz—of alcohol. The most commonly used ones in the treatment of alcoholism are naltrexone and nalmefene. Both help prevent relapse, naltrexone in low-level to moderate drinkers and nalmefene in heavier drinkers. Both drugs are more beneficial if the individual

One of the most difficult parts of ending a substance abuse problem is getting through the discomfort of physical withdrawal symptoms.

66 Chapter 3—Getting Help

Brand Name vs. Generic Name

Talking about medications can be confusing because every drug has at least two names: its "generic name" and the "brand name" that the pharmaceutical company uses to market the drug. Generic names are based on the drug's chemical structure, while drug companies use brand names to inspire public recognition and loyalty for their products.

is also receiving psychological counseling, such as cognitive-behavioral therapy.

Another type of drug used to treat alcohol abuse is disulfiram, sold under the brand name Antabuse®. Disulfiram is an *aversion drug*; it interacts with alcohol to produce very unpleasant side effects such as nausea, vomiting, and headaches. Just a half a glass of wine combined with Antabuse® can produce the symptoms, which last from one to two hours, depending on the dose of disulfiram and the amount of alcohol consumed. Studies have shown that the drug is most effective if the individual has someone around who will make sure that he takes it.

Depression frequently occurs in individuals with alcoholism and alcohol abuse problems, and depression can contribute to relapse, a serious—and likely—concern with individuals going through recovery. Often, healthcare professionals prescribe antidepressants such as Prozac® or Zoloft® to treat this depression. Though there is some evidence that antidepressants may reduce cravings for alcohol, the primary indicator for their prescription is the presence of depression.

Opioid Addiction

Medications have also proven to be effective in treating addiction to opioids such as prescription pain medications and heroin. Naltrexone, methadone, and buprenorphine are the drugs most often used in treating this addiction.

Just as it does when being used to treat alcohol addiction, naltrexone blocks the effects of opioids, including the sought-after highs.

One of the best-known medications used in the treatment of opioid addiction is methadone. Methadone is a man-made drug perhaps best known as a treatment for heroin addiction. This drug occupies the opiate receptors in the brain instead of the opioid itself, which allows an addict to stop using the drug without going through withdrawal. The drug is taken orally once a day, and works to suppress withdrawal symptoms for twenty-four to thirty-six hours. It blocks the high from the opioids, yet provides the body with the drug that it has come to depend on. However, it does not actually end an addiction; a user is still physically dependant on opioids. All methadone does is keep an addict from feeling withdrawal symptoms, as well as stopping the extreme mood swings that many addicts have as the levels of opioids in their blood rise and fall. Because it does not end the user's need for an opioid in his body, methadone is often addictive in itself and is considered a Schedule II drug.

> **FAST FACT**
>
> According to the NIDA, the average cost of one year of methadone maintenance is $4,700 per individual undergoing treatment; one year of incarceration costs approximately $18,400 per inmate.

However, addiction to methadone is seen as a better addiction to have, as the drug is safer for the patient than

The History of Methadone

Max Bockmühl and Gustav Ehrhart in Germany first discovered methadone, a synthetic chemical, in 1937. They were looking for a painkiller that would be easier to use in surgery and have a low addiction potential. In 1947, the chemical giant Eli Lilly and Company introduced the drug to the United States. It quickly became used both as a low-price alternative for treating narcotic addiction and for pain management. Methadone was sold under the name Dolophine®, which derives from the Latin words meaning "pain" and "end."

One rumor claims that the name Dolophine® was not coined because of its Latin roots, but instead was a tribute to Adolf Hitler and that the drug name was originally spelled "adolphine." While this has been proven to be false, it is still considered a fact by Scientologists. When Tom Cruise, a popular actor and member of the Church of Scientology, pointed this out in an interview with *Entertainment Weekly*, the magazine replied by pointing out the fact that the name was created after World War II by an American company with no desire or motivation for naming a drug after Hitler.

many opioids. Unlike other opioids, methadone will not cause damage to internal organs like the heart, lungs, kidneys, brain, or bones. It does not impair one's ability to think or make rational decisions, things that opioids affect. There are fewer side effects than with other opioids; potential side effects are mild and include water retention, sweating, a rash, and drowsiness. These symptoms often go away after the dosage is adjusted or once the user gets used to the drug.

Methadone has other benefits as well. For instance, the drug costs less than twenty dollars a day—compared to heroin, which can cost $3,000 an ounce. It is also a cheaper alternative to prison time, which would cost thousands of dollars in tax money. Methadone can also

Methadone is addictive and is classified as a Schedule II drug. Despite its risks, methadone treatment is a cheaper alternative to prison time.

stop the spread of HIV/AIDS, as well as other diseases that are spread by sharing needles.

Methadone is longer lasting than many other opioids, mostly because of its high *solubility* in the body's fat. The drug has a *half-life* of twenty-four to forty-eight hours, meaning that it can be taken once a day and still provide relief from withdrawal symptoms.

Levo-alpha-acetyl-methadol (LAAM) is an alternative to methadone. It has a longer half-life than methadone; those undergoing treatment with LAAM need only take the medication three times per week, rather than daily, which is the case with methadone. Individuals being treated with LAAM do not experience highs, and the sense of emotional steadiness makes it an attractive alternative to many. Some, however, find that they experience increased anxiety while on the medication, and they require additional support. One form of LAAM, ORLAAM®, was removed from the market in 2003 due to cardiac problems caused by the drug.

The newest component in addiction treatment's pharmacological arsenal is buprenorphine, approved by the FDA in 2002. Buprenorphine can be administered by a certified doctor in an office setting, negating the need for inpatient status or trips to a drug clinic or hospital to receive ongoing treatment. The drug's effects are long lasting, and it is less likely to cause respiratory distress than other medications used in the treatment of prescription painkiller addiction. Although buprenorphine was tested for ten years before receiving FDA approval, its widespread use is too new to determine its long-term efficacy.

Buprenorphine is prescribed both alone, in the drug Subutex®, and in combination with naloxone in

Suboxone®. The combination drug was designed to reduce bubrenorphine's potential to be abused by injection. These two drugs are the only Schedule III, IV, or V drugs used to combat opioid addiction. This classification means that they have a legitimate medical purpose, a low chance for abuse, and are not likely to be harmful to the user.

As an opioid partial agonist, buprenorphine produces similar effects to other opioids, even the euphoria and respiratory depression. However, it works on a much smaller scale than opioids like opium and heroin do. Because its effects are more minimal and less noticeable, the drug is used only to help addicts stop using other opioids and does not have as great a potential for abuse itself. Buprenorphine does have some side effects, many of which are the same as other opioids'. Nausea, vomiting, and constipation are all potential problems.

The clinical treatment of addicts with buprenorphine has three phases. The first is called the **induction** phase, where a user who has abstained from opioids for at least twenty-four hours (and is therefore in the early stages of withdrawal) is given buprenorphine. This stage is medically monitored; if the patient has other opioids in her system, the buprenorphine could make the body go into acute withdrawal. The second stage is the stabilization phase, when a patient no longer has cravings for the opioid. Due to the chance of side effects, the dosage of buprenorphine is often adjusted at this stage. The third and final stage is the maintenance phase, when the patient has responded well to a set dosage of the drug. Once a user is not dependant on the original opioid, there are two choices: to keep a patient on the buprenorphine indefinitely as long as she continues to do well on the drug—or to stop the drug gradually and put the patient through a

Buprenorphine was approved in 2002 for the treatment of opioid addiction. It must be administered by a certified doctor in an office setting.

Addiction Treatment—Escaping the Trap

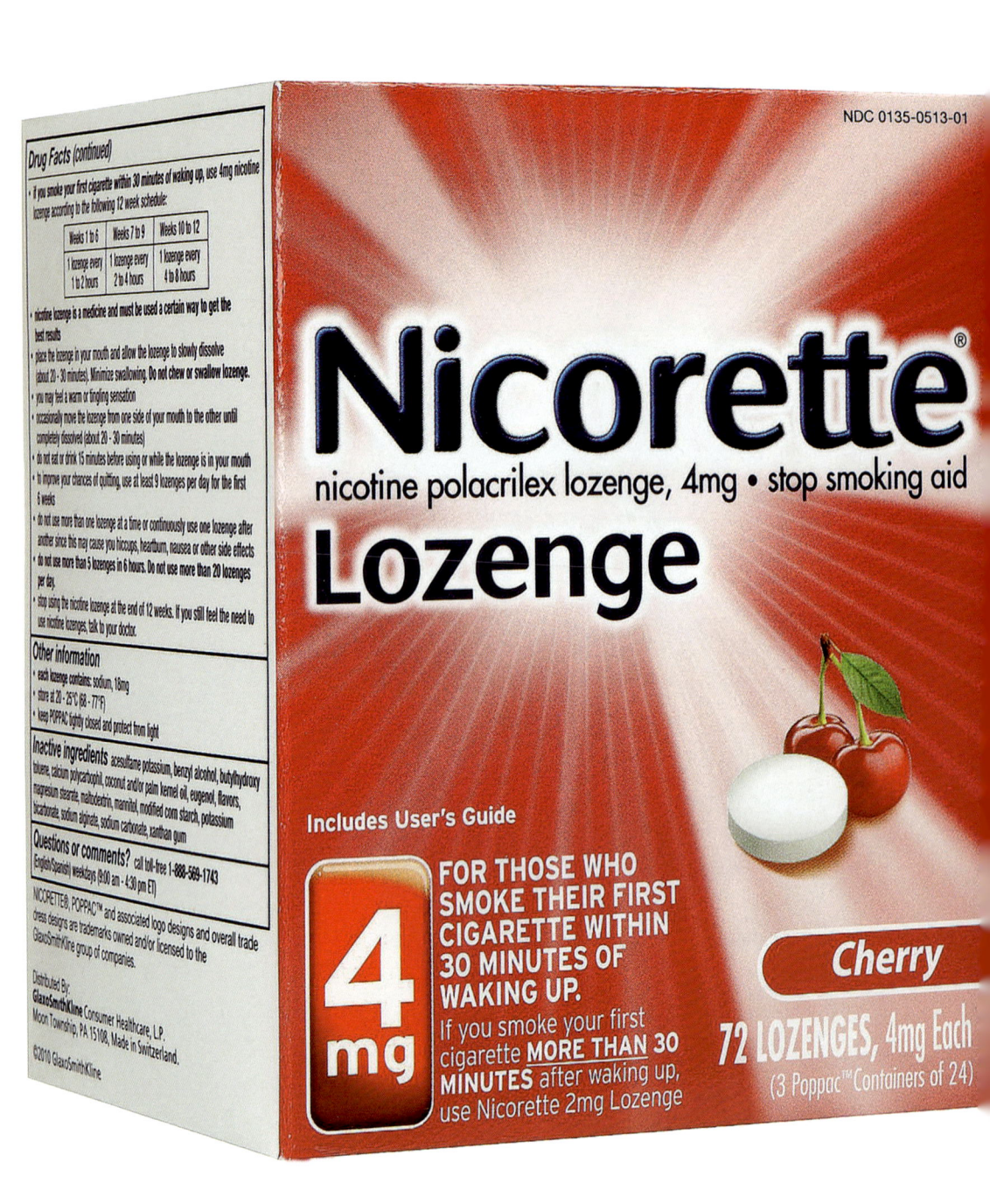

Treatments for nicotine addiction have a high success rate. Most of these products work by gradually reducing the amount of nicotine in the body.

74 Chapter 3—Getting Help

medically supervised withdrawal. While the symptoms in the second scenario will not be as severe as they would have been if the opioids were still in the bloodstream, they will last longer.

Nicotine

Research has shown that drug treatments for nicotine addiction have a high success rate. Over-the-counter availability of these medications—along with intense media messages encouraging all smokers to stop—will hopefully increase the rate of successfully quitting smoking.

Nicotine was the first drug approved by the FDA for use in smoking cessation therapy. Nicotine replacement therapies include nicotine gum, a nicotine lozenge, the **transdermal** patch (commonly called "the patch"), nicotine nasal spray, and nicotine inhaler. These are just the therapies approved in the United States and Canada; countless other varieties are being developed and sold in other parts of the world. These nicotine-replacement products are designed to ease withdrawal symptoms. They are safe alternatives to tobacco and provide lower overall nicotine levels. These products have a low potential for abuse because they provide little of the other pleasures of cigarettes. According to U.S. government research, all the nicotine-replacement products appear to be equally effective.

Cocaine

Currently, cocaine addiction has no accepted pharmacological treatments. Some drugs, however, can be successfully used to alleviate problems that come during the early days of abstinence. For example, antidepressants have been proven to have benefits for some people. Comprehensive addiction treatment programs may use any of a number of potential drugs to treat specific disorders that can accompany the addiction on an individual basis. Other individuals might receive anxiety-reducing drugs; and still others may receive a safer form of stimulant.

Each year, cocaine overdose leads to many emergency hospital admissions and deaths. To help prevent those deaths, the National Institute of Drug Abuse (NIDA) is aggressively working toward identifying and testing medications that can be used to treat cocaine abuse, thereby lessening the possibility of overdose. Some researchers

Cocaine overdose is a leading cause of hospital admissions and deaths. There is currently no pharmacological treatment for cocaine.

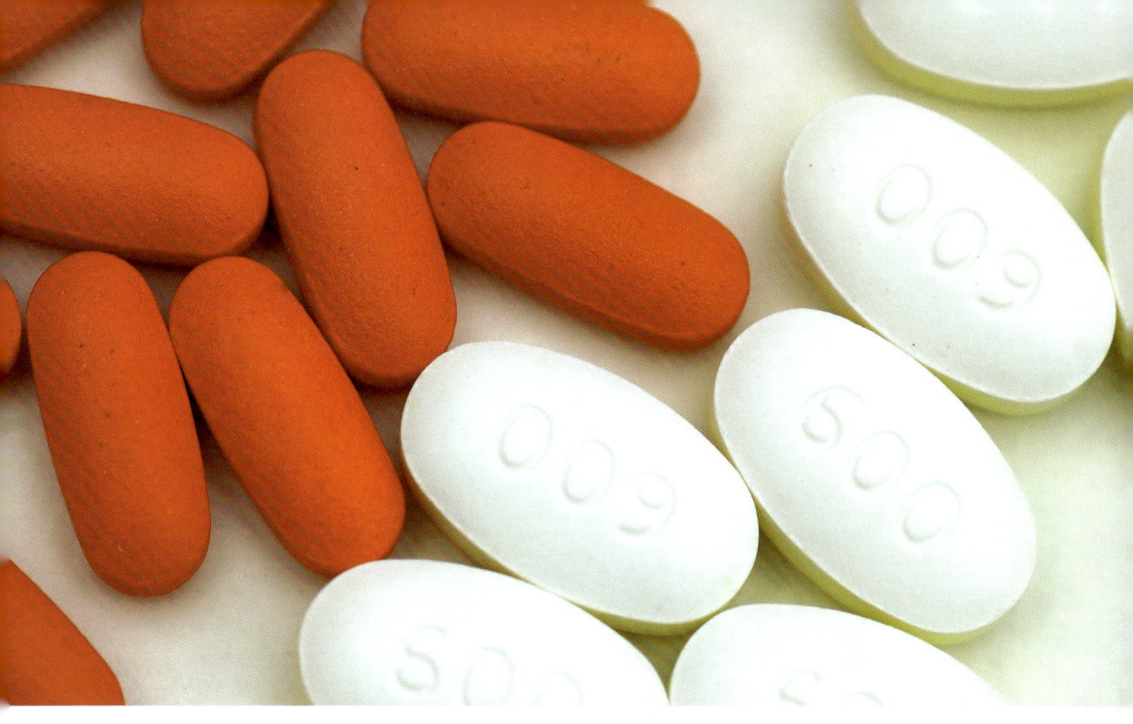

Antidepressants have proven to be effective in alleviating problems that occur in the first days of abstinence from cocaine.

are working on a vaccine that would make users immune to cocaine's effects, eliminating one of the factors that make the drug attractive.

Inhalants and Solvents

Research into pharmacological treatment methods for inhalant and solvent abuse is fairly recent. A study conducted at the U.S. Department of Energy's Brookhaven Institute in 2004 has given some hope to those looking for pharmacological help in combating this form of addiction. Scientists there found that vigabatrin (gamma vinyl-GABA, or GVG) might block the effects of toluene, an ingredient in many of the most-abused inhalants. When tested on animals that had been trained to look for toluene in certain areas, these animals did not spend as much time looking for the substance once they had received GVG. In humans, treatment with GVG

Research into pharmacological treatments for inhalant abuse is fairly new. However, there have been promising findings on the ability of vigabatrin to block the effects of toluene, a chemical found in wood smoke and many inhalants.

would hopefully reduce, if not eliminate, the desire for toluene-containing substances. As yet, however, as is the case with cocaine, no generally accepted drug treatments have proved to be effective.

Steroids

There are no pharmacological treatments for steroid addiction itself. Instead, pharmacology can play a role in treating the effects of steroid abuse. For example, anabolic steroid abuse can throw the body's hormonal balance off kilter. Many medications used to treat steroid withdrawal restore the hormonal imbalance the steroids have caused. Other medications are used to treat specific withdrawal symptoms such as headaches and muscle and joint pain. Special attention is paid to any symptoms of depression, as this is a common condition experienced by individuals kicking steroids. Should the individual exhibit symptoms of depression, antidepressants may be prescribed, along with other forms of therapy. Of course, if long-term damage has been done to the individual's body, medications and other treatments will be provided.

So far, researchers have not been able to find a pharmacological treatment for all forms of addiction. Medicine has yet to be found that can treat Ritalin® and over-the-counter medication abuse. For individuals addicted to these substances, behavior therapy is the most effective road to recovery. It can also play an important role in the long-term recovery process of even those also benefiting from pharmacological programs.

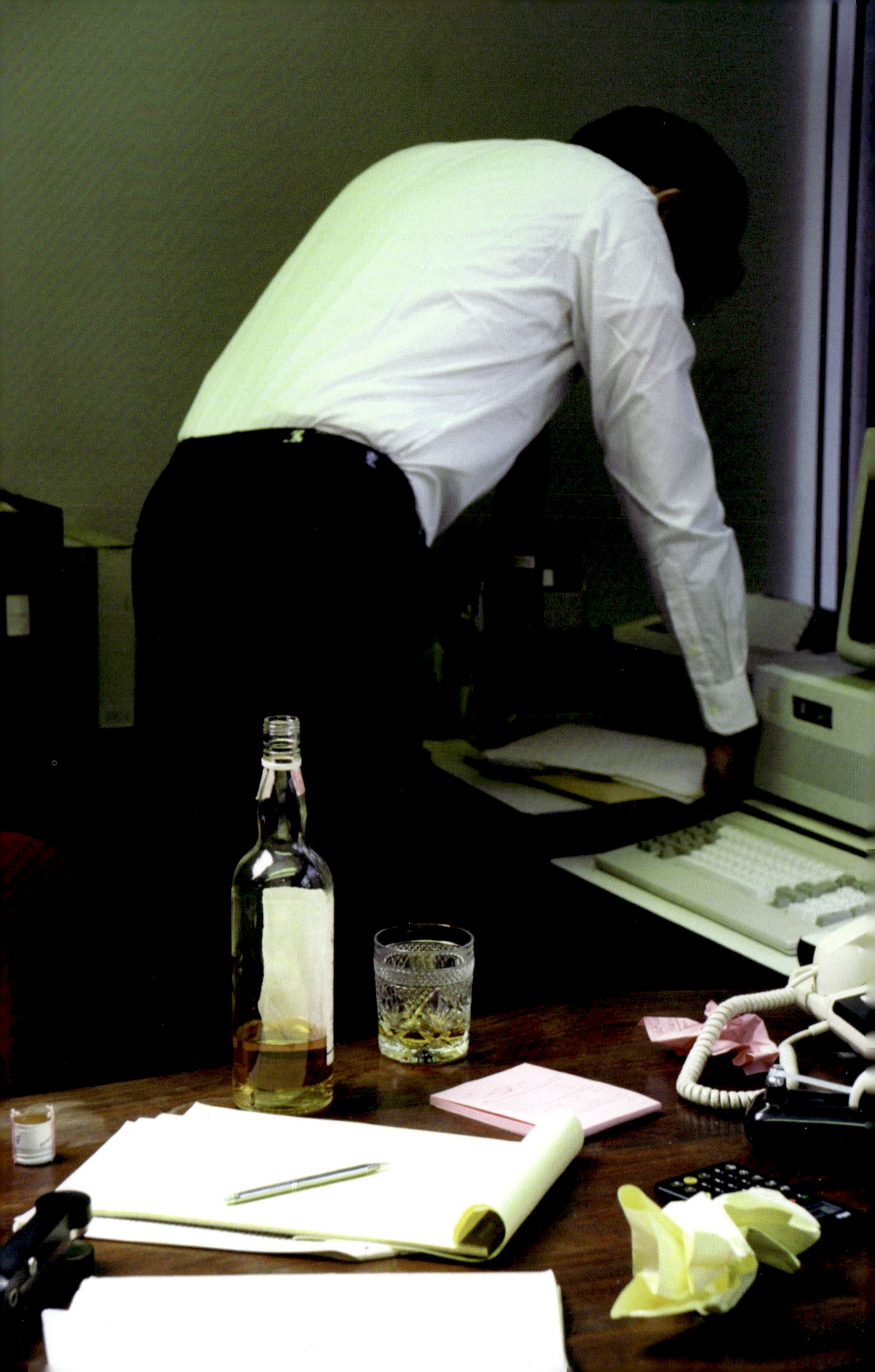

4 Beyond Drugs: Nonpharmacological Treatment of Addiction

Many individuals prefer a life of predicted patterns; that way, future events can be anticipated and prepared for. Life is pretty routine for many individuals with a substance abuse problem: get the drug, get high, crash, get the drug, get high, crash, get the drug, get high, crash . . . Not exactly a pattern that leads to a productive and successful life—at least not one recognized by most of the population.

Eventually, most individuals with a substance abuse problem do attempt to become sober. For most, the process begins with a stay in a hospital or treatment center. During the first few days, while the body goes through detox, health-care professionals use medical interventions when possible to lessen the withdrawal symptoms experienced by the individual. In some cases, that might be enough to prevent further substance use. However, experts in the field of addiction have found that by adding forms of behavior modification therapy, the chances of a successful recovery are increased. In fact, these therapies are truly the bedrock of any treatment program for addiction or substance abuse. For some addictions, drug therapies may help the process, but counseling and behavior modification programs will be essential for every individual recovering from substance abuse or addiction.

As has been discussed elsewhere in this book, the withdrawal process can be very painful; in some instances, it can even be life threatening. For this reason, the first few days of withdrawal are often spent in a hospital or treatment center. This is where behavioral treatment begins.

> **FAST FACT**
>
> Not everyone goes into treatment on her own volition. In some cases, the legal system orders that an individual undergo drug or alcohol treatment as a condition of parole or probation. According to the NIDA, individuals who undergo court-ordered treatment have just as high a success rate as individuals who participate voluntarily.

Behavioral Treatment Programs

Put simply, behavioral treatment programs teach people with addictions to change their behaviors so they are less likely to repeat those that led to addiction in the first place. Unfortunately, however, nothing about addiction is simple. Though behavioral treatment programs do help those with addictions find ways to avoid behaviors that can cause a relapse, such treatment methods also need to help individuals discover what led to those behaviors initially. Cognitive-behavioral therapy (CBT) helps the

Ideally, an individual should choose to undergo treatment. However, court ordered treatment has the same success rate as that which is voluntary.

Addiction Treatment—Escaping the Trap

individuals recognize how thought patterns influence behaviors. With therapy, individuals learn how to change negative thought patterns, and thereby change behaviors. Individual and family therapy can help the person with addiction and those around her learn how to cope with the recovery process. Therapy can also help the addicted individual and her associates handle relapses; most people do relapse at some point during recovery, and all involved need to think of these occurrences as setbacks, not failures.

Behavioral treatment programs also help those with addictions handle life without the drug or substance that has been abused, including the sometimes-painful cravings that result from abstinence. Avoiding addictive substances is not always easy or, in some cases, even practical. Take prescription painkillers, for example. Besides dealing with the physical and psychological effects of not using the medications, the individual must also learn how to deal with pain. Even if her introduction to prescription painkillers was not the result of a medical need, there may come a time when pain medications will be necessary. She needs to know how to handle that situation to lessen the possibility that she will relapse.

> **FAST FACT**
>
> As of 2010, there were more than 1,000 addiction treatment centers in Canada. Most were similar to ones operated in the United States.

Supportive-Expressive Psychotherapy

Not all addiction treatment methods are designed to last over the long term. One such method is supportive-expressive *psychotherapy*. This time-limited method has been used most effectively in the treatment of those addicted to heroin and cocaine. Supportive-expressive psychotherapy provides supportive techniques that help the person with an addiction feel safe enough to discuss the problem. The treatment also helps the individual develop expressive techniques to enable her to identify and deal with interpersonal issues that might have led to the addiction—and that result from the drug and substance abuse problem. Research indicates that when combined with drug counseling, supportive-expressive psychotherapy improves treatment outcomes for individuals with

Behavioral therapy teaches individuals how to change thought patterns and the related behaviors.

Addiction Treatment—Escaping the Trap

Supportive-expressive psychotherapy has been most effective in treating those addicted to heroin and cocaine. This method is designed to offer short-term, rather than long-term, support.

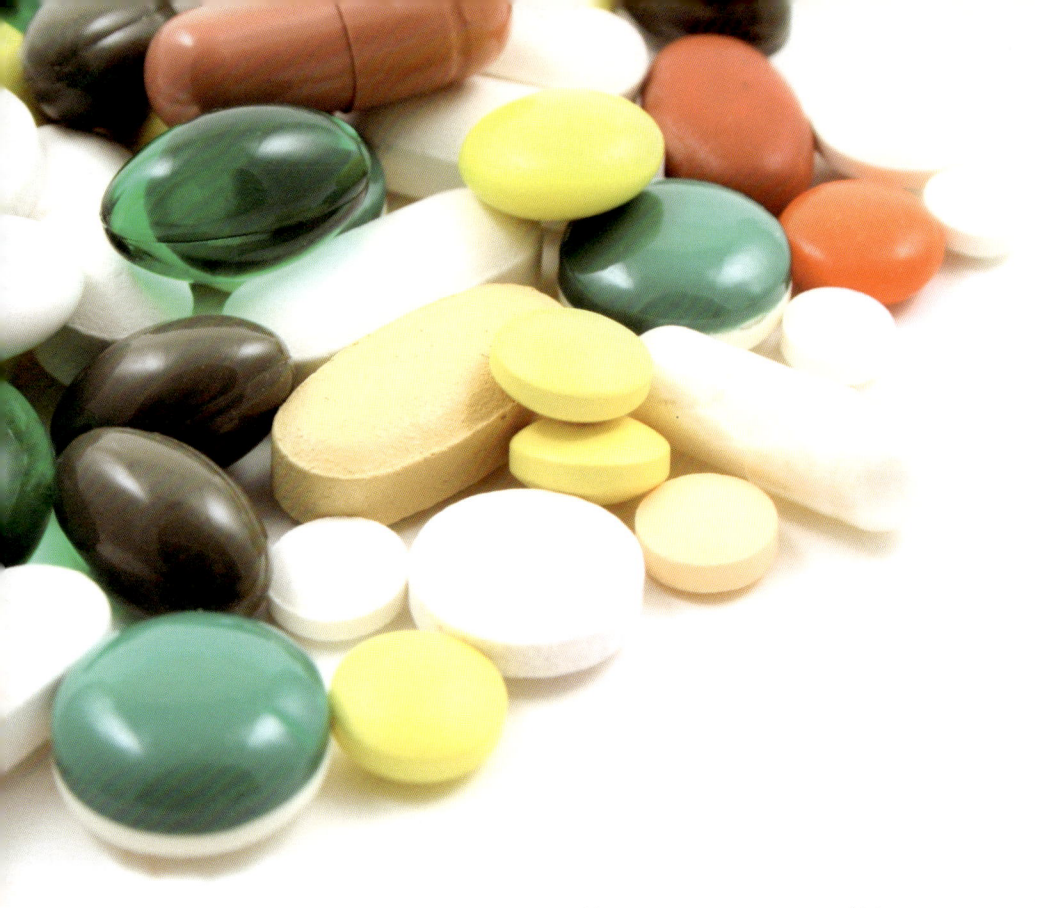

Behavioral therapy is effective on its own. However, success rates are higher when therapy is combined with a pharmacological treatment program.

concurrent psychiatric problems undergoing methadone treatment.

Motivational Enhancement Therapy

Not everyone who enters treatment is thrilled to be there. And we all know that it's easier to give our all to something we want than to something we don't. Participation in anything—including drug treatment—is perhaps even more difficult when we don't really know how we feel about it. That's where motivational enhancement therapy enters the picture.

Every difficult task is made easier with the aid of some reward as motivation. Treatment programs use motivational enhancement therapy to encourage individuals who are not sure they want treatment.

88 Chapter 4—Beyond Drugs

Treatment programs use motivational enhancement therapy when treating individuals who aren't sure they want to be in treatment, or even that they want to give up drugs or other substances. This form of therapy is relatively short term (two to four sessions after an initial assessment) and conducted one-on-one between the individual and a therapist. During the first therapy session, the therapist provides feedback on the results of the assessment tools. The individual is encouraged to talk

Just like other behavioral therapy, motivation enhancement therapy focuses on teaching the individual how to cope with situations in which he might come into contact with substances.

Addiction Treatment—Escaping the Trap 89

about the results and about his addiction. The therapist and the client work together to come up with statements that the latter can use to self-motivate his recovery efforts. As with other behavior-based treatment programs, motivational enhancement therapy helps individuals find methods of dealing with situations that put them at high risk for relapse. The remaining sessions are spent reinforcing the new coping methods and the individual's decision to stop using drugs and other substances.

Many treatment programs begin with a period of inpatient treatment. Depending on the length, severity, and drug of addiction, inpatient treatment can be short-term (usually a minimum of thirty days) or long-term residential. At first, some programs allow inpatients to have minimal—if any—contact with the "outside world." These programs help the individual concentrate on learning about herself and her relationship with the drug. Later, family and perhaps close friends are encouraged to participate in the treatment program.

Short-Term Residential Treatment Programs

Most short-term residential treatment programs were originally targeted toward the treatment of people with alcohol addiction. Twelve-step programs, devised by AA, played an integral role in treatment. The mid to late 1980s saw an alarming surge in the abuse of cocaine and other illegal drugs, and the scope of many of these programs widened to include addiction to narcotics.

Originally, short-term residential treatment was designed to provide three to six weeks of inpatient treatment at the facility. In most cases today, that is a luxury; many health insurance and managed-care plans either

Many inpatient treatment programs initially do not allow the patient to have contact with the outside world. This allows the patient to focus on learning about herself and her drug problems.

Addiction Treatment—Escaping the Trap

A therapeutic community (TC) is the best option for someone with serious addiction problems in addition to other health issues and behavioral problems. Life in a TC is very structured and therapy sessions can involve screaming and yelling.

do not cover treatment programs or severely limit the length of time one can spend in short-term residential treatment.

When an individual is released from inpatient care, he is expected to continue treatment on an outpatient basis. Counseling, both group and individual, is available at most treatment facilities or at a satellite center. Participation in support groups such as AA or Narcotics Anonymous (NA) is strongly encouraged.

Long-Term Residential Treatment Programs

Sometimes individuals going through treatment need to have access to around-the-clock care, but they do not need services found in a traditional hospital. For these people, a therapeutic community (TC) may be their best option for receiving treatment.

Individuals who are inpatients at TCs generally have more severe addiction problems. The addiction may be *compounded* by the existence of mental health issues, other physical disorders, and even criminal behavior. Despite these complications, inpatient treatment at a TC has proven to be effective for individuals with such special needs.

Individuals living in TCs can expect to spend between six and twelve months in inpatient treatment. During that time, they will learn how to live a sober life within the confines of a supportive community. Everyone involved with the TC, including treatment and support staff and other residents, plays a role in the recovery process.

Treatment in TCs is highly structured, even prison-like. Screaming and yelling often punctuate sessions, as residents are forced to carefully examine their behavior and thought processes. Old, damaging beliefs are replaced by more affirming ones. Demeaning self-concepts and low self-esteem are targets of therapy sessions, as treatment staff help the resident develop a more positive concept of herself. Job training is often provided at the TC, helping the individual learn skills necessary to live among others as a beneficial member of society.

Treatment With Special Populations

Judicially Mandated Treatment

As mentioned earlier, not everyone enters addiction treatment voluntarily. Some require an added "push," sometimes from the judicial system. The court system may **mandate** that treatment occur before, during, or instead of serving time in jail or prison. In many cases, participation in support groups is required as a condition for early release on *parole*.

Treatment programs have been very beneficial to those sent by the judicial system. They do as well or better than individuals who entered treatment voluntarily. Those who were judicially mandated to obtain treatment also tend to stay in treatment longer than others.

According to the NIDA, when treatment occurs with an incarcerated individual, research has shown that treatment is more effective when individuals are segregated into TCs away from the general prison population. This practice helps reduce or even eliminate the potentially negative influence of the **prison culture** on someone going through recovery. Most of the elements of more traditional treatment programs remain the same. Drug treatment for the incarcerated may include drug

Sometimes treatment is mandated before, during, or after prison time. Treatment for an incarcerated individual tends to be more effective when the inmate is away from the general population in a therapeutic community.

education classes, support groups (many facilities have their own AA or NA groups), and skills training.

Drug courts are a relatively new concept in dealing with increasing drug-related cases, which are clogging the judicial system. In most states, drug courts have the authority to order someone into treatment, monitor the individual's treatment progress, and help the individual obtain other services that might be needed.

Adolescents are strongly influenced by the behaviors of others. Behavioral treatment of adolescents takes advantage of this by teaching them the correct behaviors to mimic.

Adolescents

Treatment for adolescents with substance addiction centers on the concepts of model and reward. For centuries, parents have known that children and young adults are quick to copy the behaviors of others; for many people in treatment, that's how they got started using these substances in the first place. Parents have also learned that carefully considered rewards, used judiciously, can work as a great motivator.

Behavioral treatment for adolescents with substance addictions takes advantage of the **malleability** of children and teens. Role-play situations teach the adolescents how to handle themselves in situations that might cause them to resume old habits. Frequent meetings are held, during which progress toward mutually determined goals is measured. When goals are met, the adolescent receives extra privileges as a reward. To make certain that the individual is sticking to a drug-free lifestyle, urine samples are collected regularly.

Canada and the First Nations

In Canada, the treatment of inhalant abuse among members of First Nations (Native) peoples is taking a more unique approach in the National Youth Solvent Addiction (NNYSA) program. This program emphasizes resiliency in the treatment of drug addiction.

As used by those involved with the NNYSA, resiliency is defined as the extent to which someone can recover from adversity. Stories of individuals who have come back from horrendous situations are well known, but what makes some individuals able to accomplish this while others wallow in self-pity or even become criminals? According to those responsible for the NNYSA, resiliency depends on risk and shield.

Risk consists of the adverse circumstances in which an individual lives. For example, some patients residing at the White Buffalo Youth Inhalant Treatment Centre had parents who were alcoholics and who suffered from physical and verbal abuse, multiple losses, and a lack of a support network.

The individual's strengths are his shields. These strengths include personal skills, spiritual beliefs and practices, and community supports. According to proponents of the risk and shield theory, shields come from qualities inherent in the individual or from community support and from adversity itself; they can be a result of facing difficult circumstances.

The Native worldview places emphasis on one's spiritual self. North American Indians—and many non-Natives as well—believe that it is the strength, the shield, that is developed from the individual's spirit that helps one find the resiliency to rise above the bad, even to learn from it. The NNYSA treatment programs help individuals learn about their culturally based spirituality. The strength they learn to develop from their spiritual selves, combined with the shields they have inherently, can work together to help individuals achieve sobriety.

One of the major goals of therapy for adolescents is to help them develop coping methods they can use throughout their lives. These methods help the young person develop the self-control needed to maintain sobriety. Adolescent therapy focuses on two types of individual control. Stimulus control encourages the teen to avoid situations that might tempt them to use drugs, participating instead in other, more constructive activities. Urge control helps adolescents recognize the effect thoughts and feelings have on their behavior. They also learn how to challenge negative thoughts and feelings and not give in to the **deleterious** behavior they might incite.

Treatment for adolescents recognizes that teens do not live in a vacuum; family and friends play important roles in recovery. To increase the likelihood of treatment success, all behavioral treatment programs require that at least one parent or guardian be involved in the therapy. Some sessions are held with only the person undergoing treatment, others with the parent or other family members only, and sessions are held that include the individual in treatment and his support network of family and close friends. The support network can help make sure that treatment goals are met, as well as provide additional encouragement.

Outpatient Treatment

Not everyone needs the strict structure or full-time supervision provided by residential programs. For them, outpatient treatment can be a much less expensive and less disruptive option. Prime candidates for this type of treatment include individuals who have jobs and those with a very supportive social network.

Outpatient treatment may be a good option for an individual who has a job as well as strong support from family and friends.

Addiction Treatment—Escaping the Trap

Services offered through outpatient treatment vary considerably. Some simply provide drug education programs. Others facilitate group-counseling sessions. Still others operate day programs in which individuals spend the day in structured activities but go home each night. An alternative to that are programs that allow individuals to go to work or school each day, but require that they return to the facility to spend their off-work hours, including sleep. Adolescents are often treated for addiction through programs offered on an outpatient basis.

Multidimensional Family Therapy

One popular treatment method is Multidimensional Family Therapy (MDFT). MDFT treats the individual as a part of the addiction equation; family, friends, and the community also serve as variables in the individual's addiction. The theory behind MDFT is based on the idea that there is more than one way to replace negative behaviors with more positive ones.

Group and individual sessions make up MDFT treatment. When the therapist meets with the individual alone, concentration is on developing skills in decision making and problem solving. The therapist and the individual also work toward achieving effective communication skills; knowing how to express feelings can reduce the "need" to act out in more destructive ways. As in many

> **FAST FACT**
>
> The NIDA reports that conservative estimates find that there is a return on investment of between four and seven dollars for every dollar spent on addiction treatment programs. This money comes from reduced drug-related crime, criminal justice costs, and theft.

Principles of Treatment

The NIDA has come up with a list of thirteen principles that make up a good treatment program. These include:

1. *No single treatment is appropriate for all individuals.* Matching treatment settings, interventions, and services to each individual's particular problems and needs is critical to his or her ultimate success in returning to productive functioning in the family, workplace, and society.

2. *Treatment needs to be readily available.* Because individuals who are addicted to drugs may be uncertain about entering treatment, taking advantage of opportunities when they are ready for treatment is crucial. Potential treatment applicants can be lost if treatment is not immediately available or is not readily accessible.

3. *Effective treatment attends to multiple needs of the individual, not just his or her drug use.* To be effective, treatment must address the individual's drug use and any associated medical, psychological, social, vocational, and legal problems.

4. *An individual's treatment and services plan must be assessed continually and modified as necessary to ensure that the plan meets the person's changing needs.* A patient may require varying combinations of services and treatment components during the course of treatment and recovery. In addition to counseling or psychotherapy, a patient at times may require medication, other medical services, family therapy, parenting instruction, vocational rehabilitation, and social and legal services. It is critical that the treatment approach be appropriate to the individual's age, gender, ethnicity, and culture.

5. *Remaining in treatment for an adequate period of time is critical for treatment effectiveness.* The appropriate duration for an individual depends on his or her problems and needs. Research indicates that for most patients, the threshold of significant improvement is reached at about three months in treatment. After this threshold is reached, additional treatment can produce further progress toward recovery. Because people often leave treatment prematurely, programs should include strategies to engage and keep patients in treatment.

(continued on next page)

Principles of Treatment *(continued)*

6. *Counseling (individual and/or group) and other behavioral therapies are critical components of effective treatment for addiction.* In therapy, patients address issues of motivation, build skills to resist drug use, replace drug-using activities with constructive and rewarding nondrug-using activities, and improve problem-solving abilities. Behavioral therapy also facilitates interpersonal relationships and the individual's ability to function in the family and community.

7. *Medications are an important element of treatment for many patients, especially when combined with counseling and other behavioral therapies.* For patients with mental disorders who have used an illegal drug to self-medicate, both behavioral treatments and medications can be critically important.

8. *Addicted or drug-abusing individuals with coexisting mental disorders should have both disorders treated in an integrated way.* Because addictive disorders and mental disorders often occur in the same individual, patients presenting for either condition should be assessed and treated for the co-occurrence of the other type of disorder.

9. *Medical detoxification is only the first stage of addiction treatment and by itself does little to change long-term drug use.* Medical detoxification safely manages the acute physical symptoms of withdrawal associated with stopping drug use. While detoxification alone is rarely sufficient to help addicts achieve long-term abstinence, for some individuals it is a strongly indicated precursor to effective drug addiction treatment.

10. *Treatment does not need to be voluntary to be effective.* Strong motivation can facilitate the treatment process, however. Sanctions or enticements in the family, employment setting, or criminal justice system can increase significantly both treatment entry and retention rates and the success of drug treatment interventions.

11. *Possible drug use during treatment must be monitored continuously.* Lapses to drug use can occur during treatment. The objective monitoring of a patient's drug and alcohol use during treatment, such as through urinalysis or other tests, can help the patient withstand urges to use drugs. Such monitoring also can provide early evidence of drug use so that the individual's treatment plan can be adjusted. Feedback to patients who test positive for illicit drug use is an important element of monitoring.

12. *Treatment programs should provide assessment for HIV/AIDS, hepatitis B and C, tuberculosis and other infectious diseases, and counseling to help patients modify or change behaviors that place themselves or others at risk of infection.* Counseling can help patients avoid high-risk behavior. Counseling also can help people who are already infected manage their illness.

13. *Recovery from drug addiction can be a long-term process and frequently requires multiple episodes of treatment.* As with other chronic illnesses, relapses to drug use can occur during or after successful treatment episodes. Addicted individuals may require prolonged treatment and multiple episodes of treatment to achieve long-term abstinence and fully restored functioning. Participation in self-help support programs during and following treatment often is helpful in maintaining abstinence.

forms of addiction treatment, adolescents are helped to find ways of constructively deflecting negative influences and dealing with situations that might tempt them to use drugs and other addictive substances.

Family members also participate in sessions, both with and without the individual undergoing treatment. During sessions, parents are encouraged to examine their parenting styles, keeping in mind that they are the most influential people in their children's lives. Suggestions are made to help them become more effective parents, more in tune with the developmental needs of their children.

MDFT treatment sessions are not restricted to a therapist's offices. MDFT recognizes that physical setting can influence behavior. Sessions are held at family court, school, houses of worship, and other community venues.

Rehabilitation or "rehab" programs traditionally have the following basic elements:

- initial evaluation
- abstinence
- learning about addiction
- group counseling
- AA or other Twelve-Step participation
- individual counseling
- a family program

Multisystemic Therapy

Another form of outpatient treatment is Multisystemic Therapy (MST). This form of therapy concentrates on *antisocial* behaviors of adolescents with addiction problems. It does not, however, restrict the causes of those behaviors to the individual or the addiction. The role of the family, school, and neighborhood in creating an addiction-*conducive* condition are also examined.

Treatment takes place in the individual's environment. Studies have found that by locating therapy sessions within the everyday environment of the individual and her support network of friends and family, makes completion of the treatment process more likely—and completion of the MST program led to a significant decrease in drug use for a minimum of six months after the program. Successful graduates of the program were also less likely to be imprisoned or removed from the home.

Staying off drugs, alcohol, and other addictive substances while in a treatment program is one thing, but remaining sober in the "real world," with all of its challenges, is something else entirely.

What Do Rehab Programs Accomplish?

Abstinence

In many cases it seems that as long as the substance is in the blood stream, thinking remains distorted. Often during the first days or weeks of total abstinence, we see a gradual clearing of thinking processes. This is a complex psychological and biological phenomenon, and it is one of the elements that inpatient programs are able to provide by making sure the patient is fully detoxified and remains abstinent during his or her stay.

Removal of Denial

In some cases, when someone other than the patient, such as a parent, employer, or other authority, is convinced there is a problem, but the addict is not yet sure, voluntary attendance at a rehab program will provide enough clarification to remove this basic denial. Even those who are convinced they have a problem with substances usually don't admit to themselves or others the full extent of the addiction. Rehab uses group process to identify and help the individual to let go of these expectable forms of denial.

Removal of Isolation

As addictions progress, relationships deteriorate in quality. However, the bonds between recovering people are widely recognized as one of the few forces powerful enough to keep recovery on track. The rehab experience, whether it is inpatient or outpatient, involves in-depth sharing in a group setting. This kind of sharing creates strong interpersonal bonds among group members. These bonds help to form a support system that will be powerful enough to sustain the individual during the first months of abstinence.

"Basic Training"

Basic training is a good way to think of the experience of rehab. Soldiers need a rapid course to give them the basic knowledge and skills they will need to fight in a war. Some kinds of learning need to be practiced so well that you can do them without thinking. In addition to the learning, trainees become physically fit, and perhaps most important, form emotional bonds that help keep up morale when the going is hard.

(Source: *Partnership for a Drug-Free America*)

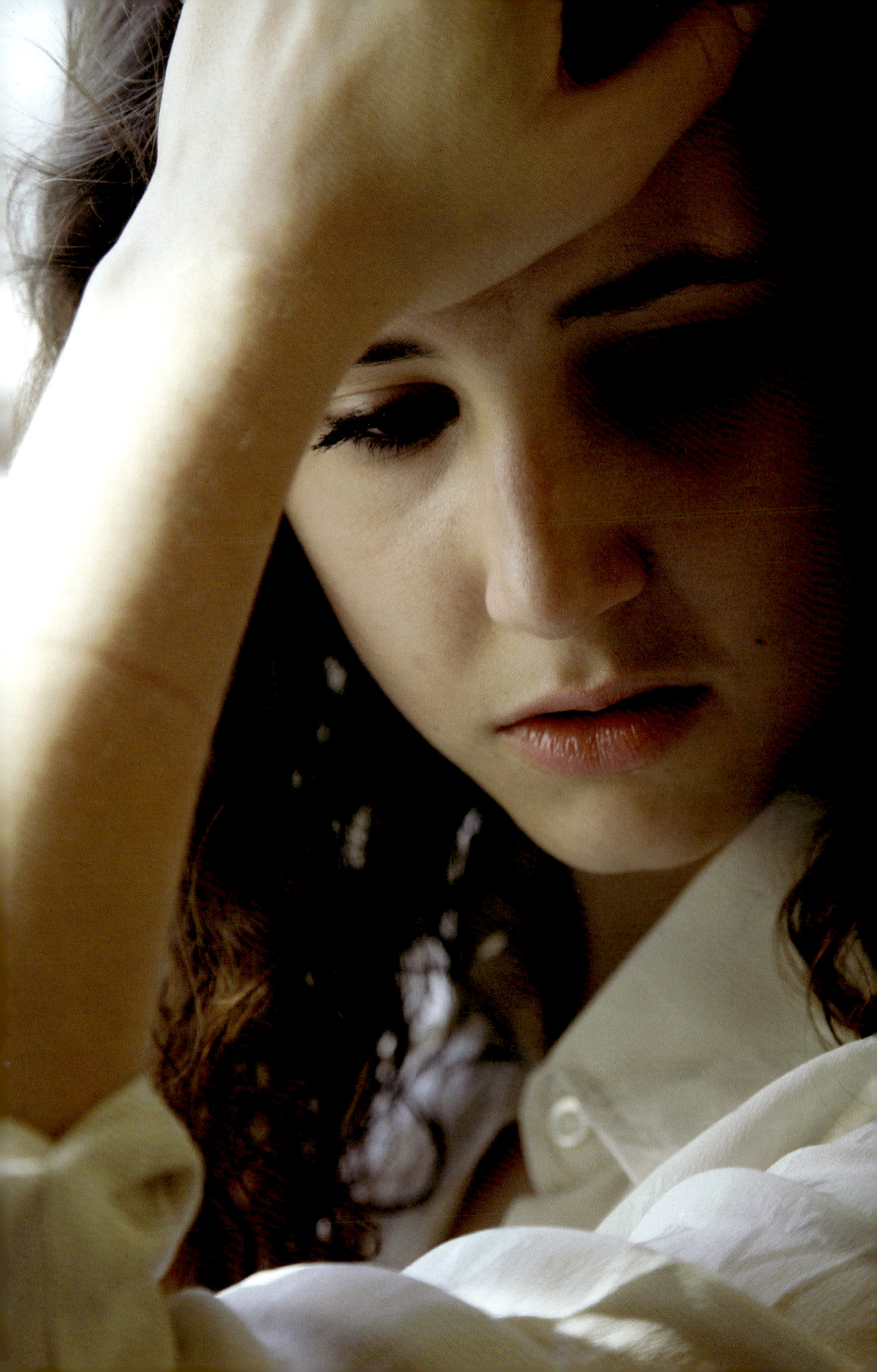

5 Staying Sober

In 2006, actor/director Mel Gibson was pulled over for suspicion of driving under the influence of alcohol. When confronted by the police officer, Gibson "went off" on a tirade. In later interviews, he admitted to falling off the wagon after more than ten years of sobriety.

The same night, actor/comedian Robin Williams entered rehab. Like Gibson, this came after many years of living a life free of alcohol and drugs. Unlike Gibson, it occurred without publicity and went unnoticed by the media until a spokesperson for Williams announced he was undergoing treatment.

When it comes to addiction, there is nothing unique about Gibson or Williams. They represent one simple fact of recovery—it is an ongoing process, which is why many state that they are recovering addicts, not recovered ones. Some experts in the treatment of alcohol and substance addiction believe that relapse should be expected in the treatment process. There are, however, methods to reduce the occurrence of relapses.

Relapse Prevention

One of the most effective ways of reducing the occurrence of relapses is cognitive-behavior therapy—CBT. As discussed in Chapter 4, CBT operates on the theory that one's thought patterns affect behavior. CBT treatment helps people recognize and change negative belief patterns that then lead to **maladaptive** behavior.

Anticipation plays a major role in relapse prevention. Effective treatment strategies help individuals learn what problems to expect and how best to deal with them, without using drugs, alcohol, or other addictive substances.

When the addiction is to an over-the-counter medication or some other easily accessible substance, the temptation to abuse can be almost overwhelming. Walking into a pharmacy, department store, or supermarket brings the recovering addict face to face with the opportunity to relapse. The development of self-control can mean the difference between relapsing or staying sober. Some treatment programs teach techniques to improve an individual's self-control. Within the context of self-control is the ability to self-monitor one's cravings and susceptibility to temptations. How can I tell that these are real cravings? Is there a particular time of day or situation that makes the cravings and temptations more intense? Are there ways to avoid tempting situations? Having the ability to answer those questions can give one the self-control to avoid many situations that might lead to relapse.

Support Groups

Sometimes it's easier to learn things—and take confrontation—from someone who has been in the same boat. It just makes sense. After all, people who have been addicted to alcohol, for example, probably know best what one feels as life changes from one centered around

Cognitive Behavioral Therapy helps to change thought patterns that lead to destructive behavior.

Addiction Treatment—Escaping the Trap

Alcoholics Anonymous is successful in part because of the importance of the group meetings. These groups act as a support system for the individual and allow interactions with other people who are struggling with the same problem.

110 Chapter 5—Staying Sober

drinking to one facing lifelong abstinence. Support groups can play a major part in helping the newly recovering as well as individuals who have been sober for many years.

The best known and one of the most successful support groups is AA. Most cities have at least one AA group, and many have multiple groups meeting in places and at times that make it possible for someone to attend at least one. NA groups are also found in many locations, but where there are none, individuals with addictions to drugs and other substances can feel at home at AA meetings.

Support groups such as AA give individuals the chance to interact with people who know what they are going through—the rough patches as well as the daily victories. They are able to provide suggestions on how to avoid high-risk situations and temptations. In addition, twelve-step programs such as AA make use of a sponsor for new members. This is someone who can be called in the middle of the night or whenever temptation strikes. Helping the newly recovering addict learn a new way of life also reinforces sobriety in the sponsor; it's a win-win situation.

Besides twelve-step programs such as AA, there are other types of support groups. Hospitals, treatment centers, and other community organizations often sponsor support groups. Some of the programs incorporate certain aspects of twelve-step programs, but many individuals find they are more comfortable in non-AA groups. People need to feel comfortable in whatever support group they choose, so they will continue to participate and benefit from the experience.

Groups like Alcoholics Anonymous have proven to be effective, but they are not the only option. Treatment centers are also run at hospitals and through community organizations.

The Internet

The Internet can be a wonderful source of information and support. And there's an e-mail list or chat group for almost everything. In-person support groups are very effective for some, but for an individual who is shy, uncomfortable about talking in groups, housebound, without transportation, or too ill to physically attend one, online groups can be a viable alternative. A March, 2012, Google search for the key phrase "online addiction support groups" returned more than 14,000 hits. E-mail lists and chat groups are also good ways to "meet" others living with the same condition. Stories about how to cope can be shared. Perhaps most important, these online support groups can help individuals learn that they are not alone in their suffering.

There are, of course, **caveats** about participating in online e-mail lists and chat groups. Although most people are honest, some people use the Internet as a way to get information about others and use it in unlawful ways. Personal information should be given out sparingly and only with extreme caution.

Care should also be taken when considering suggestions made by individuals in online groups. In many cases—perhaps most—those giving the suggestions are not experts. While it is interesting and helpful to know what has worked for someone else in recovery, that doesn't mean it will work for everyone.

The Internet is a valuable source of information. Extra support can also be found through online chat groups and e-mail lists.

Besides support groups, the Internet is a valuable source for information about addiction and addiction treatment. Again, care must be taken when reading—and believing—information. Try to determine the author and source of the information. If a business (such as a pharmaceutical company) or a particular treatment program presents the information, it may be slanted to be favorable to their perspectives. Always be on the lookout for a *hidden agenda*. Take a careful look at any dates that appear on the website, and make certain that the information is up to date. Web sites sponsored by the government are usually reliable and updated regularly.

It is important to exercise caution when using the Internet as a source of information. Some web sites may be operated by companies with hidden agendas; for example, companies out to make money on their own products.

Family and Friends

Unless one lives on a deserted island, in a hidden cave, or isolated in a home, it is almost impossible go even a day without seeing someone. For the most part, that's a good thing, because one's friends and family play integral roles in helping the individual stay sober. The family who has participated in treatment programs will learn the tools needed to be an effective partner in recovery.

The emotional health of the family members must not be ignored, however. In some cases, the person in recovery may have been addicted for many years; he may

Veterans Affairs Canada (www.veterans.gc.ca/clients/sub.cfm?source=health/wellness/9) has the following advice to individuals on how to go about changing their lives:

- **Be honest with yourself.** Does your alcohol and drug use affect your life? Your family's lives? Think about all aspects—social, physical, spiritual, economic and mental. You are the only person who can make the decision to stop.

- **Get information.** Check your local addiction services for books, pamphlets and materials. Learn how addiction develops and the stages involved in the recovery process. Knowledge will give you the understanding and confidence to help you make this change.

- **Stop using alcohol or drugs.** Get advice from a doctor or other health professional about how to safely stop using alcohol or drugs.

- **Get support.** Talk to someone about your situation, preferably someone who knows about addiction. Addiction support programs are available in every province and offer both individual counseling and group support programs. Your family and friends may also give you valuable support.

Living as a recovering addict can be almost as difficult as living with an addiction. The individual should be sure to seek the support of friends, family, and trusted professionals as she moves into a new phase of her life.

seem like an entirely new person once he has entered the recovery phase. There are support systems available to the family members of recovering addicts, and they should not hesitate to take advantage of them. Groups such as Alateen and Al-Anon provide support for children and other family members and friends of individuals addicted to alcohol, drugs, and other substances. Friends and family can meet with individuals who share the same experiences and learn ways to cope with the changing situation. Perhaps even more important, participation in such groups provides the opportunity to learn that one is not alone; others have gone through the same feelings and experiences.

The Internet can be an important resource for friends and family as well. Online support groups and e-mail lists target the needs of families and friends of recovering addicts. Websites offer information to them as well. Family and friends should also exercise the same care as recovering addicts when reading website information.

When someone is addicted to drugs, alcohol, or another substance, life can be extremely difficult. Living as a *recovering* addict can also be difficult, bringing with it a different set of problems. However, with the support of friends, families, and professionals, and those who have gone through the same experiences, recovery can be a reachable goal.

Addiction Treatment—Escaping the Trap

Glossary

abolitionism: The practice of ending slavery.

abstinence: The state of completely giving up or avoiding something.

a cappella: To sing without instrumental accompaniment.

adverse: Unfavorable or undesirable.

advocate: Someone who speaks in favor of something.

antisocial: Disliking the company of others.

aversion drug: A chemical that creates a strong feeling of dislike or hatred for another substance or situation.

beta-blockers: Drugs used to regulate the activity of the heart by suppressing the activity of beta receptors.

blood–brain barrier: A naturally occurring barrier that prevents some substances from leaving the blood and entering the brain tissue.

bromides: Chemical compounds that contain bromine and another element.

caveats: Things said as warnings or cautions.

compounded: Added to.

concomitant: Accompanying.

concurrent: Happening at the same time.

conducive: Encouraging or bringing about a good or intended result.

cortisone: A hormone secreted by the adrenal gland and used to treat rheumatoid arthritis and allergies.

deleterious: With a harmful or damaging effect on someone or something.

delusions: False beliefs held despite strong contradictory evidence.

demise: Death; end.

depth psychology: The study of the unconscious mind.

detoxification: The process of removing poison or harmful substances from the body.

efficacy: The power to produce a desired result.

endorphins: Substances in the brain that attach to the same cell receptors that morphines do, and which are released when severe injury occurs, creating a sensation of pleasure.

ether: A chemical used as a solvent and formerly as an anesthetic.

ethics: A system of moral principles governing the appropriate behavior for an individual or group.

exhorting: Urging someone to do something.

half-life: The amount of time necessary for half of a substance to be naturally removed from living tissue.

hidden agenda: A secret plan, motive, or aim motivating someone's actions.

hypothalamus: A central area of the underside of the brain that controls involuntary functions.

induction: The initial experience.

inebriate: Someone who is drunk.

maladaptive: Unsuitable for a particular function, situation, or purpose.

malleability: The ability to be easily persuaded or influenced by others.
mandate: Order; require.

methamphetamines: A form of the stimulant amphetamines.

opioid antagonists: Drugs that block the effects of opioids.

parole: The early release of a prisoner, with certain conditions.

peer group: A social group made up of people who are equal in such respects as age, education, or social class.

peptides: Chemical compounds whose amino acids have chemical bonds between carboxyl and amino groups.

pharmacology: The science of drugs.

physiological: Relating to the way living things function.

predisposition: The susceptibility to a disease arising from hereditary or another factor.

prison culture: A set of attitudes and behaviors specific to people incarcerated in prison.

Prohibition: The U.S. government's attempt to ban alcoholic beverages.

propensity: The tendency to demonstrate a particular behavior.

protocol: The detailed plan of a medical treatment or scientific study.

psychoactive: Having to do with a significant effect on mood or behavior.

psychosis: A psychiatric disorder characterized by delusions, hallucinations, incoherence, and distorted perceptions of reality.

psychotherapy: The use of psychological methods—or talk therapy—to treat mental disorders.

purgatory: In Roman Catholic belief, the place where souls go until they have atoned for their sins and can proceed to heaven.

relapse: To revert to previous behavior.

relatively: In comparison with other things.

reprehensible: Highly unacceptable.

restitution: To return something to its original condition, or compensation for loss, damage, or injury.

sectarian: Relating to or involving a particular religious group or denomination.

skepticism: An attitude marked by a tendency to doubt what others accept to be true.

sobriety: Abstinence from the use of alcohol or drugs.

social hour: A period of refreshments and socializing often held after a meeting or service.

solubility: The extent to which one substance is able to dissolve in another.

suasion: The art of persuasion or an instance of persuading.

temperance: Total abstinence from alcoholic drink.

transdermal: Something that is introduced into the body through the skin.

travails: Troubles, hardships.

Further Reading

Blume, Arthur W. *Treating Drug Problems*. New York: Wiley, 2005.

Diamond, Jonathan, and David Treadway. *Narrative Means to Sober Ends: Treating Addiction and Its Aftermath*. New York: Guilford Press, 2002.

Durham, Michael. *Painkillers and Tranquilizers*. Portsmouth, N.H.: Heinemann, 2003.

Levin, Jerome D. *Therapeutic Strategies for Treating Addiction: From Slavery to Freedom*. New York: Jason Aronson, 2001.

Padwa, Howard, and Jacob Cunningham. Addiction: A Reference Encyclopedia. Santa Barbara, Calif.: ABC-CLIO, 2010.

Peele, Stanton. *7 Tools to Beat Addiction*. New York: Three Rivers Press, 2004.

Pinsky, Drew, and Todd Gold. *Cracked: Putting Broken Lives Together Again*. New York: HarperCollins, 2004.

Stevens, Patricia, and Robert L. Smith. *Substance Abuse Counseling*. Upper Saddle River, N.J.: Prentice Hall, 2004.

For More Information

Addictions.org
www.addictions.org/signs.htm

Adolescent Substance Abuse
www.drug-addiction.com/adolescent-substance-abuse.htm

Dealing with Addiction
www.kidshealth.org/teen/drug-alcohol/getting_help/addictions.html

Drug Rehab
www.drug-rehab.com/teens.htm

Drug Rehab Treatment
www.drugrehabtreatment.com

Drugs and Teen Substance Abuse
www.focusas.com/SubstanceAbuse.html

Teen Drug Abuse
www.teendrugabuse.us/resources.html

The websites listed on this page were active at the time of publication. The publisher is not responsible for websites that have changed their addresses or discontinued operation since the date of publication. The publisher will review and update the website list upon each reprint.

Bibliography

"Addiction and Alcoholism—Definitions and Strategies." http://www.recovery-man.com/addiction.htm.

"Addiction Treatments Past and Present." http://learn.genetics.utah.edu/units/addiction/issues/treatments.cfm.

American Association of Oriental Medicine. "Acupuncture and Addiction." http://www.aaom.org/default.asp?pagenumber=4802.

Clinebell, Howard J., Jr. "Understanding and Counseling the Alcoholic." http://www.religion-online.org/showchapter.asp?title=576&C=726.

Daniels, W. H. *The Temperance Reform and Its Great Reformers*. New York: Nelson & Phillips, 1878. http://www.eskimo.com/~burked/history/daniels.html.

"Do You Have a Drug or Alcohol Problem?" http://www.recovery-man.com/trouble.htm.

Drucker, Ernest. "Where Is the Addiction Field Headed?" *Cross-Current—The Journal of Addiction and Mental Health*, December 22, 2003.

Lipton, Douglas S. "Therapeutic Communities: History, Effectiveness and Prospects." *Corrections Today*, October 1, 1998.

National Center for the Advancement of Prevention, Center for Substance Abuse Prevention. "What Is Addiction? From Decision to Disease." http://preventionplatform.samhsa.gov/macro.csap/dss_portal/portal_content/addictionta/addiction.ppt?CFID=484569&CFTOKEN=6-749130.

National Institute on Drug Abuse, National Institutes of Health. "Principles of Drug Addiction Treatment: A Research-Based Guide." http://www.nida.nih.gov?PODAT/PODATindex.html.

Office of National Drug Control Policy. "Treatment." Washington, D.C.: Author.

Orange, A. "The Religious Roots of Alcoholics Anonymous and the Twelve Steps." http://www.orange-papers.org/orange-rroot030.html.

White, William L. "Addiction Treatment: Gone Yesterday, Gone Tomorrow?" *Behavioral Health Management*, September 1, 1999.

Index

adolescent treatment 98–100
Alcoholics Anonymous 40, 59–64, 97, 113
alcoholism 68, 69

behavior modification 84–86, 109, 110
blood-brain barrier 16
buprenorphine 73–75

cocaine 77–79

dependence 13
detoxification 67
Diagnostic and Statistical Manual of Mental Disorders (DSM) 18, 20
drug courts 97

Emmanuel Movement 49–59
endorphins 16

Federal Food and Drug Administration (FDA) 27

Harrison Anti-Narcotic Act of 1914 59
history (of addiction treatment) 37–65

Internet 114–116, 119

judicially mandated therapy 96, 97

Keeley Cure 58

LAAM 73

methadone 70–73
motivational enhancement therapy 89–92

multidimensional family therapy 102, 105
Multisystemic Therapy 105

National Institute on Drug Abuse (NIDA) 70, 84, 103–105
nicotine 77

Opioids 69–76
Oxford Group 61

pharmacology 13, 67–81
prescription drugs 20
psychoactive drugs 16
psychotherapy 86–89

rehabilitation 107
relapse 110, 111
residential treatment 92–96
Rush, Benjamin 39, 42

Salvation Army 46
steroids 81
stress 25
support groups 110–113
symptoms (of addiction) 28, 30

temperance 40, 44
therapeutic communities 95, 96
Therapeutic Product Directorate (TPD) 27
Twelve Steps 59, 62–64

Washingtonian Movement 40–48
withdrawal 16, 18
Women's Christian Temperance Union 45, 47

Picture Credits

DEA, http://www.usdoj.gov/dea/index.htm: p. 11
Dilsiz, Mehmet: p. 21
fotolia.com: pp. 12, 16, 73, 83, 87, 89, 91
    Michal Adamczyk: p. 8
    Joachim Angeltun: p. 22
    Yuri Arcurs: p. 31
    Arvind Balaraman: p. 77
    Adam Booth: p. 95
    Robert Byron: p. 27
    Masca Cosmin: p. 17
    Lyle Doberstein: p. 76
    Christopher Ewing: p. 30
    Philip Lange: p.
    Morgan Mansour: p. 78
    Thomas Mounsey: p. 86
    Anita Patterson Peppers: p. 19
    Peter Spiro: p. 24, 112
    stockphotonyc: p. 91
    Leah-Anne Thompson: p. 20
    Michael Thompson: p. 113
    Lisa F Young: p. 85
istock.com: pp. 64, 106, 116
    Abimelec Olan: p. 96
    Emrah Turudu: p. 114
Jupiter Images: pp. 15, 34, 36, 39, 41, 50, 53, 60, 61, 62, 66, 70, 80, 92, 109, 110
Library of Congress: pp. 45, 46

To the best knowledge of the publisher, all other images are in the public domain. If any image has been inadvertently uncredited, please notify Harding House Publishing Services, Vestal, New York 13850, so that rectification can be made for future printings.

Author and Consultant Biographies

Author

Ida Walker is a graduate of the University of Northern Iowa in Cedar Falls, and has done graduate work at Syracuse University in Syracuse, New York. The author of several nonfiction books, she lives in Upstate New York.

Series Consultant

Jack E. Henningfield, Ph.D., is a professor at the Johns Hopkins University School of Medicine, and he is also Vice President for Research and Health Policy at Pinney Associates, a consulting firm in Bethesda, Maryland, that specializes in science policy and regulatory issues concerning public health, medications development, and behavior-focused disease management. Dr. Henningfield has contributed information relating to addiction to numerous reports of the U.S. Surgeon General, the National Academy of Sciences, and the World Health Organization.